To Romany, who once told me a very funny story
about a toddler and some bubbles

CANDY HARPER

KEEP the FAITH

SIMON AND SCHUSTER

First published in Great Britain in 2014 by Simon and Schuster UK Ltd
A CBS COMPANY

1 3 5 7 9 10 8 6 4 2

Simon & Schuster UK Ltd
1st Floor
222 Gray's Inn Road
London
WC1X 8HB

Simon & Schuster Australia, Sydney
Simon & Schuster India, New Delhi

A CIP catalogue record for this book
is available from the British Library.

PB ISBN: 978-0-8570-7825-4
EBook ISBN: 978-0-8570-7826-1

Printed and bound by CPI Group (UK) Ltd, Croydon, CR0 4YY

www.simonandschuster.co.uk
www.simonandschuster.com.au

DECEMBER

MONDAY 26TH DECEMBER

I can't wait for the New Year to begin. This is the year I will take action and use my intelligence and initiative to follow my dreams. For example, today I have pursued my ambition of being warm and cosy in this draughty old house by using my skills to build an igloo out of duvets.

Of course, like many truly brilliant people, I am held back by non-believers. Lots of the world's most successful types have suffered abuse and hardship, setbacks and ridicule. I know just how they feel: my parents won't buy me a laptop. I told them quite frankly that their Christmas gifts will not help make me an international success. My hippy mother said, 'I want you to spend less time hooked up to something electronic and more time communicating with your family.'

'If I had a laptop, I could message you all.'

She scowled at me in a way that I think is pretty aggressive coming from someone who wants to save newt habitats.

Anyway, I actually did spend several minutes of yesterday communicating with my family. Even my slimy little brother who I usually avoid speaking to. I gifted Sam with several expressions of good cheer. I said, 'This is a traditional Christmas Chinese burn,' and, 'What sort of rubbish present do you call this?' That kind of thing. There were also some instructions about fetching me the chocolates and altering the volume of the TV. I hope he was grateful for my festive friendliness. I'm not planning on speaking to him for the rest of the year.

Granny came over for Christmas dinner, which was quite a lot of work. Obviously, I didn't do any actual cooking, but just being in the same room as Granny is quite tiring. She's always throwing herself around and babbling on about her latest boyfriend, when really she's at an age where it would be more appropriate if she just sat in a corner handing out sweets and money while wearing a skirt that actually covered her wrinkly knees. The energy I spent blocking out her singing and dancing to 'Santa Baby' left me utterly washed out. Which means I will have to leave working towards my other dreams for another day. For now, I'll stay in my igloo and catch up on some texting while eating the candy canes from Sam's stocking.

TUESDAY 27TH DECEMBER

All this Christmas business of communicating and loving and giving and not karate-chopping your family has been distracting me from what is really important in life: how incredibly popular I am with the boys.

At the after-show party for the Christmas choir concert I had a good time chatting to my hilarious friend, Ethan, and then I had a spectacular time snogging gorgeous Finn. I'm sort of sure that Ethan asked me to Ryan's New Year party and I am totally sure that Finn sent me a text asking me to the same party.

I have no idea where that leaves me.

I replied to Finn and said I would love to go with him, but I can't exactly remember what I said to Ethan as I wasn't completely listening to him when he was talking ... I think it might have been, 'Mmm.' That's not really a yes, is it?

LATER

I rang my bestie, Megs.

When she picked up, I said, 'Could you stop selfishly being at your cousins' house?'

'Hello, Faith. Happy Christmas to you too. I had a lovely day. Oh yes, some ace presents, how sweet of you to ask.'

I allowed her to blabber on. Part of being a good friend is listening to your mates' nonsense. I let her go on for several sentences and I hardly yawned at all. Eventually, I interrupted to say, 'Can we get back to me? I need to know when you're coming home.'

'Why? Can't you live without me?'

'It's more that when you spend a few days away from me you start getting out of hand.'

'I'm coming back tomorrow.'

'Great. Make sure you get an early start because I'm expecting you at my house by lunchtime.'

WEDNESDAY 28TH DECEMBER

Megs finally showed up around three. Even though she was late, I couldn't help smothering her with kisses. I hate it when she goes away. 'I've missed you!' I said, squeezing her round the middle.

'Get off, you gigantic potato head!'

Which I took to mean that she had missed me too.

'That's enough of your sweet talk,' I said. 'Let's get down to business. As you know, we're here to discuss what I should do about me accidentally having two dates to Ryan's party.'

I may have turned a few pirouettes at this point.

Megs tutted. 'Faith, I don't think that you're taking this seriously.'

'Yes I am. I'm completely serious. It is a very serious business when all the boys around you fall helplessly in love with you.'

And then I did a somersault on my bed.

'Faith!'

'What? That was a *serious* somersault. I thought

that it might dislodge some good ideas from my brain.'

Megs flicked at my duvet. 'I think that all it's dislodged is some dandruff.'

Which was rude, but I have to make allowances for her. She was probably lashing out because she's so jealous.

So I only kicked her in the shins a little bit.

Megs said, 'I'm not jealous. I've got a boyfriend. All you've got is two invitations to a party and we're not even sure if one of them actually happened.'

'What do you mean you're not jealous? Who said you were jealous? I never said that.'

'No, but you've been singing "Megs is a green-eyed monster".'

I hadn't realised that I was doing that out loud. Just goes to show that I still haven't got my mouth fully under control. How can I be expected to snog with these disobedient lips?

'Sorry,' I said. 'You should ignore the things that come out of my mouth that I don't mean to say.'

'How am I supposed to know which ones they are?'

I shrugged. 'Just assume that I don't mean anything that makes you mad.'

Megs blew out a long breath. 'What are you going to do then? Who do you want to go to the party with?'

I threw myself back on the bed. 'Finn, of course.'

'Why?'

'Because he's gorgeous!'

Megs pursed her lips. 'You used to think Ethan was fit.'

'He is, but not like Finn. Come on! You stared at Finn the first time you met him.'

'Maybe. I'm not that keen on him now. I think he loves himself a bit. I don't like people who know how good-looking they are.'

'He can't help being good-looking and I don't think he's vain about it.'

'Do you know who's not vain and also a good laugh? Ethan.'

I realised what Megs was trying to do. 'Does this have anything to do with Ethan being your boyfriend's best friend? Are you trying to persuade me to go out with Ethan so that we can go on dates with you and Cameron? Can you not bear to be separated from me?' I put her in a headlock and ruffled her hair.

'Yep,' she said in a slightly gaspy voice. 'I just can't get enough of this.'

I let her go. 'I really like Ethan. I just like Finn more.'

'Are you sure he really likes you? He's always chatting up girls.'

'That's just talking. He's friendly. That's why I like him.'

'Yeah, that and his cheekbones.'

I bashed her with my pillow. 'I would like to let Ethan down gently and go to the party with the cheekbones; do you think you could support me in that decision?'

'If that's what you want.'

So we ate Sam's chocolate Santa while we tried to think of what I could do about my excess boy problem. I'd only got halfway through a leg when Megs said, 'Why don't I just tell Cam to tell Ethan that you're going with Finn? Problem solved and we don't have to worry about you speaking to anyone and messing things up.'

It did seem to sort things out, but I couldn't help being a bit disappointed. I don't know why. Obviously, I hadn't been enjoying agonising over two lovely boys who both seem to find me irresistible. And clearly Finn is my number-one choice to go to the party with.

Isn't he?

'So now can we talk about something more important?' Megs said. 'What are we going to wear to the party?'

'I suppose,' I said. 'But we might have to go over the nightmare of Ethan and Finn both adoring me one more time later.'

Megs made a harrumphing noise, which I took to mean she was looking forward to it.

THURSDAY 29TH DECEMBER

Today Megs, Lily, Angharad and I went into town to go sales shopping for new clothes for Ryan's party. I got up incredibly early (10 a.m.) so that we'd have plenty of time. As I was fuelling up on Pop-Tarts and Sam's box of Celebrations, Mum started delivering her speech on the evils of chain stores. She said, 'You've just been given lots of lovely things for Christmas, Faith. I don't understand why you need to go pouring more money into the big companies' pockets.'

'I'm helping the economy,' I said.

Mum sighed. 'You're such a capitalist. Wouldn't you rather use your money responsibly by buying ethically sourced products? We've got some lovely things in the shop at the moment.'

I know the sort of thing they sell in the shop Mum manages. It's all hand-carved this and yak wool that. I would not describe any of it as lovely.

'I *will* be using my money responsibly,' I said. 'Imagine what would happen if I stopped shopping. If Topshop and New Look had to close down, there would be hundreds of skinny girls out of a job and they're not qualified to do anything else. They wouldn't last a week on the streets! They've got no body fat!'

Mum shook her head.

'Now if you'd like to make a donation to my charitable shopping trip then I'll be on my way.'

When we got into town, it was heaving with people.

'Why are they here?' Megs asked.

'Maybe they want to buy stuff too?' Angharad suggested. Angharad has both the nature and the stature of a kitten. She's tiny and always thinks the best of people, even the ones that are clearly idiots because they're annoying me.

'None of them can be doing anything as important as finding an outfit for Ryan's party so they should all have some consideration and go home,' Megs said, elbowing an old man out of the way.

'The problem with shopping is that there's a lot of shop and I'm only one girl,' I said. 'If I was magic, I'd command the best possible outfit to come flying out to me now and then I wouldn't have to spend three hours looking for it.'

Actually, it took five hours in the end. But I have definitely bought the best miniskirt that ever existed.

LATER

I tried to explain my skirt-finding triumph to Mum, but she was unmoved. I'll remind her of this the next time she tells me that I don't share my life with her.

FRIDAY 30TH DECEMBER

We went to Granny's house for lunch. I say 'lunch', but there was just a lot of cold turkey and pickle and crackers and cheese and mince pies and nuts and jelly sweets. I don't call that lunch. That's a snack at best.

'What have you been up to, Faith?' Granny asked.

'Not much.' I don't know why we have to spend so much time with Granny over Christmas. All this family time gets in the way of the true meaning of Christmas, i.e. eating chocolate with my friends.

'Don't you want to know what I've been up to?' Granny asked.

'Is it something gross like rubbing moustaches with one of your ancient boyfriends?' I picked up the glass bowl of Quality Street from the coffee table.

'Faith! I haven't got a moustache.'

'Not yet,' I said.

Granny leant over and snatched the bowl out of my lap.

'If you want me to keep quiet, you should probably leave those there,' I said, grabbing a purple one as she whisked them away.

But Granny didn't care about me going hungry. She put the Quality Street on the highest shelf and said, 'I went to a lovely party at Max's house.' As if I was interested. 'He gave me this!' She opened a drawer in her dresser and pulled out a mobile phone. It was still in its box.

'Aren't you going to open it?' I asked.

'I thought I'd wait for your father,' she said, jerking her head towards Dad who had already fallen into a half-coma in front of the TV. 'I don't want to give myself an electric shock.'

I snorted. 'Why do you think Dad knows anything about mobile phones?'

'Well, he had a walkie-talkie that time he worked in the warehouse, didn't he?'

'It's not the same thing, Granny.'

'It's similar.'

'Not really.'

'Perhaps I'll ask the man in the hardware shop then.'

Dad looked up from the TV. 'Ask Faith,' he said. 'Her phone spends so much time in her hand, sometimes I think she'll grow skin round it.'

'But she's a child!' Granny said. 'She shouldn't be operating machinery. What about the radiation waves?'

My whole family decided to ignore this remark. I don't know why Mum worries about whether we're close enough. We're clearly of one mind when it comes to Granny's lunacy.

I took the phone out of the box and tried to get Granny started.

By teatime, we'd only got as far as texting.

'But why isn't there a button for every letter?' Granny moaned.

'There are on some phones,' I explained in an extremely patient way, 'but the buttons are titchy and it would annoy you.' A lot of things annoy Granny.

'Why can't they be big then?' she asked. 'Like a computer.'

'You wouldn't want to carry that around in your handbag, would you?'

'Oh, I don't think I'll take it out,' Granny said. 'I don't want to lose it. I think I'll just keep it in its box.'

I banged my head against the coffee table. 'It's a *mobile*,' I said. 'You're supposed to take it out. That's the point.'

Granny shook her head. 'I'm not sure I could walk and talk at the same time,' she said, as she walked towards me.

I rolled my eyes. 'I know that multitasking is a bit tricky for your generation.'

Granny stuck her tongue out. 'I can do these things at the same time,' and she jammed a

New Berry Fruit in her mouth with one hand and smacked me round the head with the other.

By the time we got home, I was shattered. Educating old people is tiring. I won't be giving any more of the elderly lessons in modern living. Their brains are not compatible with the technology.

SATURDAY 31ST DECEMBER

I stayed in bed for as long as possible this morning. Dad came barging in at midday and asked me why I was still under the duvet.

I said, 'I'm conserving energy for tonight.'

'You've spent so much time in that bed this holiday that you ought to have saved enough energy to run a marathon and power a fridge on wheels to keep your Lucozade in.'

'Marathon runners don't drink Lucozade,' I said.

'That's not really the point I'm making.'

'Isn't it? Have you thought about some kind of flash cards? I think they'd help with letting us poor normal people understand what's going on in your crazy head.'

I haven't got any more time to write down the rest of Dad's random dribblings. I'm going round to Megs's house with Ang and Lily so we can all get ready for Ryan's party together, and I've got to pack up my stuff. I might have to borrow Mum's wheelie suitcase for my make-up.

JANUARY

SUNDAY 1ST JANUARY

I love New Year. I can't help thinking that I'd enjoy it more if we lived in a mansion and the butler set off fireworks at midnight, but last night was pretty amazing.

Let me start from the beginning. Me, Lily and Ang got to Megs's house early. Before we started getting ready, we had a steadying Coke and a fortifying piece of Christmas cake or three. There was a lot of squealing and dancing, and Lily, who is nearly as strong as she is crazy, attempted to do the lift from *Dirty Dancing* on a hiccuping Megs, but after a while I noticed that Angharad didn't seem to be entering into the spirit of things.

I said, 'What's the matter, Ang? You're a bit quiet. We've normally had at least a couple of half-syllables from you by now.'

'That's it,' Ang said. 'I'm too quiet, aren't I? That's why boys aren't interested in me.'

'You're not *that* quiet. There was only that one time that I had to check your vital signs to make sure you were still alive.'

Then I saw that Ang was not in a jokey mood. 'Don't worry about it, sweetie. Elliot from choir seemed pretty keen on you. After all, not everyone likes girls as shouty as Megs and Lily.'

Megs made some choking noises and seemed to

be pointing at me. Lily threw an empty Coke can at my head. I can't think why.

'It's not just the chatting,' Ang said. Her little face was all creased up. 'Why would Elliot look at me when I hang around with you lot? Lily has got, you know ...' She waved her hands about in front of her chest.

'Got what?' I asked. 'Bad taste in jumpers?'

Ang shook her head.

'An inability to do her buttons up? What?'

'*You know*,' Ang said, turning scarlet.

'I think she's talking about her womanly figure,' Megs said.

'Do you mean my boobs, Ang?' Lily asked. 'Is that it? Boobs? Are you saying that I've got big boobs?'

'Stop saying that! Stop saying ... that word.'

This was a pretty harsh attack coming from Ang, so we all stopped saying anything at all for a moment.

Ang took a big breath. 'Megs is pretty and Faith is a red-headed vixen and Lily's ... developed *and* she's gorgeous.'

We all took a good look at Lily's lovely figure and beautiful face.

Lily picked a bit of foil out of her teeth.

I said, 'You think I'm a red-headed vixen?'

'Yes,' Ang said. 'And I'm just ...'

'When you say vixen . . .'

'Faith!' Megs jabbed me in the middle. 'We're talking about Angharad. Ang, you're adorable.'

'That's another way of saying I'm short, isn't it?'

'No, it means you're pretty,' Lily said.

I nodded. 'And you may be on the petite side, but that's not a bad thing. Lots of people would be jealous of your daintiness.'

'Really?'

'Yes,' I said. 'And my mum says that we should all be proud of our bodies and what makes us individual and special.' I was rehashing the speech that Mum gives me whenever I complain about the weird elbows she's passed on to me, but Angharad gave a small smile, so it seemed to be working.

I followed it up in the car on the way to the party by saying, 'Remember that you're a lovely person as well as pretty and my granny would kill to have your tiny bottom, so embrace your petite-y-ness and seize the moment with Elliot, yeah?'

'Embrace and seize.' She nodded. 'Got it.'

But once I'd selflessly raised Ang's confidence I started to feel a bit nervous myself. What if Finn didn't turn up? The last text I had from him said, **See you there**. But I didn't even ask him what time because I didn't want to sound like my dad.

When we got inside, I felt a bit better. The whole house was covered in Christmas decorations and the place was packed. There were loads of Radcliffe boys I recognised from choir, plus a lot of Year Tens and Elevens from our school, including Becky and Zoe who sit behind me and Megs in Maths. There were also a handful of girls from St Mildred's. I reckon that the entrance requirements for that school are that you've got the face of an angel and the heart of a demon. The first person we saw when we pushed our way into the kitchen was Cherry.

'Oh no. Tell me it's not her,' Megs hissed under her breath. She still hasn't got over her beloved Cameron almost attending the Christmas Fayre Cherry organised. Megs really knows how to hold a grudge.

'It's not Cherry,' I said. Because you know me, I like to oblige my friends whenever I can. 'It's a giant-sized Barbie. People are always confusing the two.'

'She'd better not try to get her plastic hands on Cam.'

On the kitchen table there was an impressive array of party food. I started to wonder whether Ryan's parents had noticed that I'd borrowed a couple of slices of bread and a bit of squeezy cheese last time their son had a party. Actually, that was a pretty special sandwich. I managed to squirt squeezy cheese on Finn and that was how we had our first proper chat. I wonder if Finn thinks of me when he walks past the cheese section in the supermarket.

'Wow,' Lily said, slipping Hula Hoops on to her fingers like rings.

'Yep,' I said. 'It's a pretty good spread I've got them to put on for you.'

'It's amazing how you think everything starts with you,' Megs said.

'I don't think *everything* starts with me,' I said, giving her a poke in the ribs, 'just all the good stuff.'

Angharad obviously agreed with me because she distracted Megs by saying, 'Look, they've got cheese and pineapple.'

I do like food that comes on a cocktail stick. I was particularly impressed that Ryan's mum had gone the whole hedgehog and covered an orange in foil and stuck the cheese and pineapple sticks in that.

No one was really tucking into the food so I thought I'd do the host a favour and get things started. I had some crisps, some grapes, a few cheese and pineapples and then finished up with a handful of mint Matchmakers for their breath-freshening effect.

After that, we went to mingle in the sitting

room and then Cam arrived and Megs dragged me over to him. It's so annoying the way that people who have boyfriends are always saying hello to them when they see them. Ethan was with Cam so, while the happy couple were getting all greetingy, we were left staring at each other. It's hard to know what to say to someone who you think you might have agreed to a date with and then got your best friend to tell their best friend to tell them that you're going to the party with someone else. So I went with: 'Have you seen the cheese hedgehog?'

Which I think is a polite remark suited to any social occasion.

Fortunately, it turns out that Ethan also has happy memories of cheese and pineapple.

He said, 'At a party, when I was little, I stuck all the cocktail sticks from my cheese and pineapple into the jelly and th—'

I missed what he said next because a pair of arms the size of pythons went round me and someone bounced me up and down vigorously.

'Faith!'

It was Westy, Ethan's friend and my favourite bear-shaped boy.

'Do you like my new trainers?' he asked, waving his size elevens in my face. 'I reckon I look sporty.'

'They look great, Westy.'

He seemed pleased that I liked them and

grinned really hard at me for quite a long time. I wondered if I was supposed to say something else, but Ethan clapped him on the shoulder and said, 'I was just telling Faith about Ben Dobbs's fifth birthday party. Remember when I spiked the jelly with cocktail sticks?'

'Yeah, I still tried to eat it, didn't I?'

I could well believe it; I've seen Westy knock back a family-size packet of super spiky crisps like a glass of water.

We all chatted for a bit until someone insisted Westy went outside to have his photo taken with the inflatable snowman in the garden. To be fair, the resemblance was pretty strong.

I asked Ethan how his Christmas was.

He ran a hand through his shiny black curls. 'Oh, you know how it goes: Aunt drinks too much, Aunt decides she needs a holiday, Aunt books a flight to Hawaii using your mum's credit card, Mother pulls Aunt's hair out. Same old, same old.'

I laughed. 'At least when my granny is on the sherry she restricts her embarrassing behaviour to the confines of musical theatre.'

'My aunt normally goes in for looking at photos of herself as a child and crying about where it all went wrong. This was a new departure. I think she's moving in the right direction.'

'So who gets to go to Hawaii?'

'Clearly, I was the obvious choice.'

'Clearly.'

'Unfortunately, my mum loves money more than her only child so, instead of rewarding me for spending Christmas in the company of shouting adults by giving me a little holiday, she managed to get a refund.'

'Madness,' I said.

'This is why I enjoy talking to you, Faith. I like the way you think.' He smiled and I felt a warm bubble expand in my tummy. He leant closer to me and said in a confidential voice, 'Of course, that's mostly because the way you think is the way I think. If you had plastic surgery to look like me, I'd probably have to marry you.'

My tummy bubble popped and sent off fireworks and swirls of confetti. *Whoa*. I was supposed to be on a date with Finn (even though I was starting to wonder where the monkey he'd got to). I'm not sure that Ethan should have been setting off a street party in my middle section just because he was joking about marrying me. I pulled myself together. I'd actually been chatting to Ethan for quite a while now and Finn still hadn't arrived. I told Ethan I needed to talk to Lily and went off to look for Finn.

By now, the house was crammed with people. I saw Lily playing Twister with some boys, but

I didn't even get a glimpse of Angharad. By the time I'd done a tour of the whole house, the only interesting thing I'd found was my arch-enemy Vicky Blundell (AKA Icky) standing in a laundry basket while snogging a boy with long hair. I've got no idea why. I mean, I don't know why she was standing in the basket, not why she was snogging the boy. (Although, to be honest, he was pretty greasy, so that was a questionable call too.) I'll just say I wouldn't let Icky rummage around in either my mouth or my dirty washing. Anyway, I didn't find Finn or any of the boys I used to see him sitting with at choir. I was starting to think I'd been stood up.

I went back downstairs to find Ethan talking and smiling with some ridiculously pretty Year Eleven girl. They both turned round when I walked into the crowded kitchen and I didn't want to look like I was desperate for Ethan's attention, so I pretended I'd just come in for a snack. I grabbed the nearest thing on the table, which happened to be someone's leftover paper plate with four cocktail sticks, half a poppy-seed cracker and a pickled onion on it.

'There it is!' I said out loud and then I attempted to slink off before anyone noticed that I seemed to be the only person at the party not talking to an attractive member of the opposite sex.

The thing about pickled onions is that they're not really designed to sit still on a plate, especially if the plate is moving. As I walked towards the door, the onion started to roll. I tried to stop it falling off by tipping the plate back towards me, but unfortunately my hand caught on the back of a chair and I ended up flicking the plate pretty hard. The onion flew across the room – catching everyone's attention – and landed in the curly hair of a very unimpressed-looking boy.

I probably should have left the party straight away, but for some reason I thought I could make things better by retrieving the onion. I nipped over to the boy, who was staring at me in disgust, and reached out a hand towards his head. 'I'll just ...' At this point I realised that, other than the music coming from the sitting room, the kitchen was completely silent. '... Get this and ...' It was a bit of a struggle because his hair was really thick and the onion was pretty slippery, but finally I had it.

The boy said, '*Thanks.*' But what he obviously meant by that was, 'Get away from me, evil-onion-girl, and don't go dragging me into your inability to look cool at parties.' Which I thought was a bit rich from a boy who was wearing a bright yellow shirt, but I had other matters on my hands. More specifically, I had a pickled onion on my hands. I didn't really know what to do with it so I popped it back on my plate. Leaving me exactly where I started. Glancing up, I saw Cherry and a black-haired friend sniggering at me. They weren't the only ones. That's what happens if you draw attention to yourself in such an oniony way.

Finally, I scuttled out of the kitchen door, this time with the sides of my paper plate curled up to stop any further runaway-snack disasters. I can only hope everyone was so mesmerised by what an idiot I am that they didn't whip out their phones and take pictures.

Out in the relative quiet of the hallway I realised that I was actually starving hungry. I wasn't going back in the kitchen so I was forced to eat the half-a-cracker. Which still left me with the plate and the onion. Before anyone else walked by and saw me with my stinky little vegetable friend, I pushed the plate through the banisters and left it on a stair next to an abandoned paper cup.

I was about to hunt out Ang and Lily when there was some banging on the front door. Since the snogging couple standing next to it didn't seem to hear, I brushed the crumbs off my top and opened it. It was Finn and his friend Josh.

Finn said, 'Faith!' and he sounded so pleased to see me that I forgot about how long I'd been waiting for him to arrive.

Josh disappeared into the throng. Leaving me face to face with Finn. He was wearing black jeans and a black top. It made his hair look incredibly blond. He gave me a smile like the sun coming up and said, 'I totally forgot about tonight.'

Well. That's not a good sign, is it? If he really liked me, surely he should have been counting down the minutes like I was. But then he did say, 'I mean, I didn't forget the party and that, but I forgot that tonight was tonight and my mum was like, aren't you going out for New Year?'

So he didn't forget the party 'and that'. What is 'and that'? Am I 'and that'? It doesn't sound very flattering. I didn't really know how to respond so I just smiled, and then I remembered the cracker and panicked that my teeth were full of tiny black poppy seeds. I tried to smile without showing my teeth which must have looked a bit creepy because Finn said, 'You OK?'

And I said, 'Yep, yep, yeah.' Which sounded like a cheerleader, but he didn't seem to mind.

I really wanted to go and check my teeth, but I could see the queue for the loo was now snaking down the stairs and it seemed foolish to abandon lovely Finn, especially as I'd just spotted Icky circling nearby. I tried to think of something intelligent to say. After a long pause, I came up with, 'How was your Christmas?'

'Yeah, wow, Christmas is crazy, right?'

Christmas had been pretty crazy in our house, mostly because Granny had too much Baileys and then decided to revisit her role as Rizzo in the over-sixties performance of *Grease*. But I was pretty sure that Finn wasn't talking about that so I said, 'Crazy?'

'Yeah, all that tinsel hanging about. I nearly strangled myself twice.'

I could imagine that. Finn isn't much of a one for looking where he's going.

'I love all that stuff you get on the telly though,' he said. 'Did you see that programme with the kid who makes the snowman? Then he's, like, an elf working for Santa?'

He told me a lot more about this great film. I'm pretty sure that he fell asleep during one film and woke during the next. But it was nice listening to him talk about how much he loves snow and presents and, well, pretty much everything really He's so nice.

Then we had a dance. I impressed myself with my multitasking by managing to shimmy my way over to the tree and sneaking a look at my teeth in a very shiny bauble. They were thankfully poppy-seed free and snog-ready. Then we had a drink and Finn wolfed down some crisps. I was feeling a bit fluttery in the stomach again, so I just nibbled on a chocolate biscuit or six.

While we were in the kitchen, talking to Becky and Zoe (I did most of the talking – Becky and Zoe mostly gawped at my gorgeous date), there was the unmistakable *thud duh-duh-duh-duh dunk* of someone falling downstairs. People were whooping and cheering so I assumed that the person who'd tripped didn't need an ambulance.

'Ow!' came Westy's voice down the hall. 'Who left that slimy little devil there?'

I pulled Finn into the sitting room before anyone could point the finger at me.

Anyway, Westy could just as easily have been talking about Icky as my pickled onion.

Cam and Megs were in the sitting room so we sat with them. (Megs managed not to tell Finn that he's too good-looking or anything stupid like that.) Then Lily made us all do some silly dance her pen pal had told her about.

Soon it was approaching midnight and there still hadn't been any kissing. I was starting to wonder if I'd got the wrong end of the mistletoe and that we weren't really on a date. Then I remembered my lecture to Angharad. If I wanted a snog then why shouldn't I stride out there and get one?

At a couple of minutes before twelve someone turned off the music and switched on the telly. I managed to grab the tiny sofa in the corner for me and Finn. Most of the people in front of us were standing up, trying to get a good look at Big Ben on the TV, so it was quite private really.

This was it. I was going to start the year as I meant to go on. The minute that clock started chiming, I was going to grasp the slippery pickled onion of destiny and snog that boy. Everyone started counting down from ten. I took a deep breath. The clock struck; all around us people were jumping up and down. This was the moment.

Before I went for it, I'd planned to say Finn's name to make sure I had his attention – I figured you don't want someone swerving their head at the last minute. That might result in ear kissing, and no one wants that. But I didn't have to say Finn's name. Everyone else was squeaking and squealing the New Year in, but Finn was looking right at me with this big grin on his face so ... I leant in. And he leant in too. I was so relieved that I almost laughed, but that could have turned into unpleasant spluttering so I got a grip. His lovely soft lips pressed up against mine while party poppers were going off all around us. It was fantastic.

Or at least it was until I realised that sitting side by side on a sofa is not the best position for kissing. I tried to turn my body towards him, but it was hard to do without putting my knee up on his leg and that seemed a bit forward. So, with my knees still facing front, I twisted my upper body as far as I could. It was not comfortable. That's when it occurred to me that I hadn't been concentrating on my technique at all. My mouth had been kissing away without me. For once in my life, I was thankful that my lips have a mind of their own.

When I managed to forget about the rest of my body and live in my lips, it was amazing. It got quite passionate and mouths were opened. Finn tasted of Coke. Just as I was wondering what the polite way to end a snog is, he slowed it down and finished with a sort of peck kiss. Like a snogging full stop. I may have been a bit blinky and dazed. Cameron helped bring me back to earth by whooping in my ear.

He winked at Finn and said, 'Having a New Year snog, are we? Hey?'

Finn put his arm round me and said, 'Uh-huh.'

'Oh right.' Cam was obviously expecting more of a reaction than that, but Finn just grinned at him. 'Er . . .' Cam opened and shut his mouth. 'Great. Carry on.'

But we didn't carry on. Finn had started playing with the streamers everyone was throwing about and I was trying to ignore the death stares of Cherry and her black-haired friend. They were clearly feeling intimidated by my great beauty and impeccable taste in boys.

Megs, Lily, Angharad and me had a New Year group hug. Someone switched the music back on and it seemed like everyone in the house started dancing like crazy. Eventually, Finn tapped me on the arm and yelled above the music, 'Hey, Faith, Josh's dad is picking us up soon.'

I said, 'Oh.' I wanted to chat about when I'd see him again, but I sort of wanted him to say that he wanted to see me again first.

'Come here,' he said. And pulled me out of the crazy dancing scrum and through into the empty dining room. It was dark except for the fairy lights on the Christmas tree. It was very romantic. Finn said, 'Your hair smells nice.'

Which is a super compliment.

'What shampoo do you use?' he asked me.

I hesitated because I didn't think we had time for me to explain my haircare regime. It's quite complicated. But then Finn pointed at some tiny baubles on the tree and said, 'Do you think those are chocolate?'

We were standing facing each other, almost nose to nose, and since he didn't seem to be that bothered about me actually answering questions, and since we were FINALLY in a comfortable position for kissing, I decided to use my lunging powers again. I had already parted my lips, and we were just about to make contact, when there was a fierce '*Rrrrr RRRRRrrrr*' from under the Christmas tree and I flinched, teeth first, into Finn's left eye. I'm ashamed to say that, instead of enquiring after Finn's poor bitten eyeball, I leapt on to the table before the vicious tree-dog could attack me.

Then I realised that there was no dog. Only Angharad and Elliot squished up in the shadow under the tree, where I hadn't noticed them, making ferocious dog noises. Except they'd stopped the barking and were now killing themselves laughing.

'What the hell did you do that for?' I asked.

Angharad and her tiny friend couldn't answer because they were still laughing so much. Then Angharad inhaled a pine needle and it all got a bit hectic. Elliot started fumbling about, trying to find his pocket first-aid manual, and Finn was still looking around for the imaginary dog, so it was left to me to get down from the table gracefully (actually, I landed on Elliot's toe) and whack Angharad on the back until the pine needle came flying out and landed in a spitty blob on Elliot's arm. Fortunately, judging by the impressed look on his face, Elliot seemed to take this as further evidence of Angharad's long list of talents.

Finn woke up a bit and said, 'Hey! That was

you two pretending to be a dog, wasn't it? Pretty cool.'

Josh appeared in the doorway and Finn really did have to go. He gave me a quick kiss on the lips and said, 'Happy New Year, Faith.' And disappeared with Josh.

After that, I did a bit more dancing and had a bite to eat, but to be honest I hardly noticed polishing off the rest of the cheese and pineapple hedgehog. Or what was left of the biscuits. Or the ice cream that I found in the freezer. Because all I kept thinking was that if someone kisses you, several times, in two different locations, on different days then it can't possibly just be a huge mistake, can it? There's only one conclusion: Finn likes me.

When it was time to go, Westy gave me a goodbye hug that was so long and squashy that I was worried everyone would get to see all that cheese and pineapple again, whereas Ethan barely even bothered to say 'bye', but I didn't let that spoil my mood. While I was floating my way home (in Lily's mum's car), I asked Angharad, 'Was it just me that you scared to death with your Rottweiler impression?'

And she said, 'Oh no, we were there for most of the night. I did what you said, Faith. I embraced my elfishness and I seized the moment with Elliot.

I said, "Elliot, we're both quite small – do you want to hide under the tree and pretend to be a barking dog?" And he said he did.' She smiled a big smile. 'That was probably the best party of my life, Faith.'

Which just goes to show that people are looking for different things in a night out.

'What about you?' she asked. 'Did you have an amazing time with Finn?'

'Yep. He's so sweet and tanned and nice. Also, a fantastic snogger.'

When I got home, Mum and Dad were still up with the sad old couple they'd invited round so that they could all be sad and old together. I allowed them to give me New Year kisses (Mum and Dad, not the other ancient people – I don't encourage that sort of thing, otherwise, before you know where you are, you're expected to kiss any old blood relative) and then I went to bed and thought about Finn.

MONDAY 2ND JANUARY

Finn hasn't texted me. He's probably forgotten that I exist again.

TUESDAY 3RD JANUARY

Mum forced me to waste one of my last days of the holiday by insisting that I go into town and help Granny buy a cover for her phone. It took us most of the day to find her one she likes (pink with crystals). She bought me lunch as a treat. (I think things must have been very hard in the olden days when my granny was young because I can't think of any other reason for describing a cheese roll as 'a treat'.) When we popped to the loo afterwards, my phone went off. I thought that it might be Finn so I had a quick look; it was from Granny. It said, **No paper in here, pass some over.**

She was in the cubicle next to me.

This is what you get when you mix the elderly with technology.

WEDNESDAY 4TH JANUARY

School starts again tomorrow. Finn still hasn't called.

Fortunately, I don't need a boy to have a good time so I went to the cinema with Megs. We bumped into Ethan and Westy coming out as we were going in.

Westy said, 'What are you going to see, Faith? If you need someone to hold your hand in the scary bits, I could come in with you.' He grinned. 'And if you're going to get a snack don't bother with their popcorn – it's mostly air.'

Westy gabbled on, but Ethan said nothing. He just gave me this long look and eventually said, 'Hello.'

I don't think anyone has ever made me blush just by saying hello before, but there's something so intense about Ethan. Sometimes I feel like he's looking right inside my head. I hope he can't really do that because I may have been thinking about what lovely dark eyelashes he's got.

'Are you two meeting anyone?' Westy asked. 'Or has Finn gone surfing? Or is it too cold for that?'

'I think he's gone mountain biking,' I said. I didn't really have a clue where he was, but I didn't want to admit it.

Ethan turned away. 'All this talk of sport is bringing out the pizza lover in me. Let's get lunch, Westy.'

'Don't you like surfing?' Megs asked him.

'Nope, I'm allergic.'

'What to?' I asked.

'Exercise.'

'I see.'

'Also, bright sunlight, wetsuits and dimwits who say "dude".'

Before I knew what I was doing, I said, 'You don't like Finn, do you?' because it was obvious he was being rude about him.

Ethan raised an eyebrow. 'Oh, I don't know. Why wouldn't I like the golden-haired, angel-voiced idiot-boy who gets all the girls?'

I gave him my best frosty silence. I'm not going

to pretend that I've never laughed at Ethan's rude remarks before, but I don't appreciate him slating my sort-of boyfriend.

Westy wanted to watch the film again with us, but Ethan clearly didn't fancy it so Westy gave in and they went off to get something to eat.

Obviously, I wasn't bothered.

LATER

Westy did invite me, Megs, Ang and Lily round to his house to watch a film with the boys on Sunday afternoon. I just hope Ethan keeps his insults and his impressive eyelashes to himself.

THURSDAY 5TH JANUARY

I had to get up at the crack of dawn to go to school. I did ask Mum to write me a letter saying I'd be unable to do PE because the vegan rubbish she feeds me has left me with weak bones that are liable to snap, but she said no. I tried to explain all this to our PE teacher, Killer Bill, but she said unless I had a note I had to play rugby.

I said, 'Well, Miss Williams, I will struggle on with my noodle limbs, even though fast movements are torture to me, but you'll only have yourself to blame when I attempt a tackle and it causes my fibula to break. I expect the bone will tear through my skin and, once it's protruding, I'll probably slip and accidentally spear Lizzie through the abdomen with it, pinning her to the frozen ground.'

Killer Bill just sniffed, but I noticed that Limp Lizzie avoided me for the entire game.

Actually, if I have to do PE then rugby is probably one of the least annoying options. Normally, in sport I'm always being told to put people down and not to be so violent. Those things are completely allowed in rugby.

At least they are the way I play it.

FRIDAY 6TH JANUARY

I've got a text from Finn! He said he had a good time at the party. I said me too. We went back and forth for a bit and then he asked if we can get together tomorrow. I'm meeting him at Juicy Lucy's. I wonder which of my shoes are best for smoothie drinking.

SATURDAY 7TH JANUARY

I had a really good time with Finn today. He's just so nice. At one point we both had our hands on the table, holding our smoothie glasses, and then somehow the backs of our hands ended up touching. I had no idea that my hand had such a capacity for electric activity. I thought it might burst into flames.

We talked about going back to school. Finn's not that keen on school. He finds it hard to concentrate. I asked him if he ever sits in class planning the decapitation of his teacher. He gave me a bit of a funny look and said, 'Mostly I just think about surfing, or sometimes what I'm going to have for lunch.'

His favourite subject is PE. As you know, I'm not the biggest fan of sporting activity, but I have to say that Finn's muscly legs seem to be doing very well on it. Obviously, I couldn't actually see his legs because he was wearing jeans, but as we were pushing back our chairs and getting up to leave his calf rubbed against mine and, I'm telling you, there were some serious muscles under there. Also, it's possible that his jeans had been dusted with some sort of girl-melting powder because I almost had to sit back down again while my molecules pulled themselves together.

We walked back through the little green square near school and there was no one about. There was some kissing under a tree. Finn tasted like strawberries. He was literally delicious. It was an ace day.

LATER
Although the 'g' word still hasn't been mentioned.

LATER STILL

And for once I mean 'g' for girlfriend not 'g' for ginger. Does he not want me to be his girlfriend? Is this keeping it casual? I don't think I'm really a casual sort of person.

I once wore a prom dress to a garden centre.

SUNDAY 8TH JANUARY

Me, Megs, Ang, Lily, Ethan, Cam and Elliot all went round to Westy's house to watch a film. Westy's mum seems like the kind of tolerant, non-speaking, snack-bearing parent I have always wished for. She didn't make the ridiculous amount of fuss that other people do when a pack of teenagers turn up in their sitting room.

Once his mum had done the decent thing and got out of our way, Westy put on what he called a sci-fi classic. I'm always a bit suspicious when people describe things as a classic. I remember when my Auntie Joyce had a classic car. As far as I could work out, that meant you had to push it everywhere instead of driving it like a proper car.

I've also heard Granny described as a classic.

The film was set on a spaceship and there was a lot of stuff about an impending alien invasion. I was more interested in the romance between the captain and the chief engineer, but it's hard to concentrate on people snogging on the screen when there are people snogging in your ear. Megs and Cameron have got no shame. They've certainly got some skills though. I thought Megs would bite Cam's tongue off when I threw a cushion at her head, but they didn't even open their eyes.

Lily and the boys were riveted by the film so Ang and I had a whispered chat on the armchair we were sharing.

She said, 'How was your date with Finn?'

I grinned. 'It was fantastic. Delicious.'

'You could have asked him to come and watch this.'

Then we cracked up because we couldn't really see why anyone would want to watch it. I thought about Finn. He probably would have said yes if I'd asked him to come, but somehow Finn doesn't seem to fit in with this little group. I struggled a bit on New Year's Eve to bring him into our conversations.

'How are you getting on with Elliot?' I whispered.

Ang jabbed me in the ribs, but Elliot was too engrossed in a disruption in the space-time continuum to notice that we were talking about him.

'Really well,' Ang said in a voice so low that I practically had to lip-read. 'Earlier, he asked me what my favourite noble gas is.'

'Wow,' I said, unsure what the correct response to this kind of announcement was.

Ang and Elliot's romance is not a conventional one.

We went back to watching the terrible film. Most of the special effects seemed to have been done with toy spaceships on strings.

When a robot on wheels with bits of egg carton for eyes rolled on, I started to laugh.

'Watch it, Faith!' Westy said. 'No sniggering. This is a chilling vision of the future.'

'What, where the robots take over the earth and steal our egg boxes?'

Then there was a space battle with a lot of shooting. Lily and Westy were beside themselves with excitement. Elliot and Ang had disappeared into the kitchen and Megs looked like she was in danger of disappearing into Cameron's mouth. I found myself looking at Ethan. Who happened to be looking at me.

I had decided to let his comments about Finn go. After all, it must be hard for other boys being compared to someone as gorgeous as Finn. So, in a spirit of kindness, I was going to say something hilarious about how the fashion on other planets always seems to be stuck in the seventies, but I didn't. I just stared. And he stared back. Along with his lush lashes he's got very sultry eyes. I didn't know if we were having a staring competition or if it was more ... you know.

Elliot came back into the room and said, 'Ew, gross!'

I looked away quickly, but fortunately Elliot wasn't talking about Ethan and me staring at each other; he was pointing at the alien that had just exploded on-screen, leaving blue slime all over the spaceship.

LATER

But I probably shouldn't be having lingering stares with boys who aren't my nearly-boyfriend, should I?

MONDAY 9TH JANUARY

Last term, my evil head of year, Miss Ramsbottom, said that Megs and I were too badly behaved to be in a class together and moved me to a different tutor group. I spent the whole of last term being super good. Well, parts of last term anyway. And it was the parts where Miss Ramsbottom was watching me so that's what counts, isn't it? And she said she'd think about moving me back, but we've been at school for three days now and no one has said anything about me returning to Mrs Hatfield's tutor group to be with Megs again.

I was thinking about speaking to Miss

Ramsbottom about it, but then Lily got out her lunch. It was a Christmas selection box. I felt that, as a friend, I ought to stick around and eat her Freddo for her while she concentrated on more caramelly options. But I will definitely be having words with Ramsbottom tomorrow.

TUESDAY 10TH JANUARY

Adults are so uptight. If Angharad doesn't mind me dangling her over the banisters, I don't see why anyone else should care. Unfortunately, Mr Hampton, our Science teacher, can only cope with people who are the right way up and walking in straight lines, so he tapped me on the shoulder (which isn't really a wise thing to do to someone who's concentrating on not dropping their tiny friend on her head) and told me to go and see Miss Ramsbottom. Pigging hell, why are teachers always sending you to see other teachers? Or making you stand somewhere or telling you to think about something. It's like they imagine you haven't got any plans of your own for the day.

I said, 'It's a nice idea, Mr Hampton, but actually I've got some important birthday business to conduct in Maths next lesson, so I don't think I'll be able to make it.'

Mr Hampton said, 'Never mind then – you mustn't upset your schedule.'

Or at least that is what he would have said if he lived in Sane World, but because he is a teacher from the planet Fun-Spoil he just ranted away. I didn't catch all of it, but it was along the lines of, 'Irresponsible ... idiotic ... most disrespectful young lady I've ever met.'

You know, the usual.

I shuffled off to see Miss R. As soon as I walked in the door, she screwed up her nose as if my behaviour smells like Bovril.

'Faith,' she snarled. 'I intended to speak to you.'

They say that attack is the best form of defence so I said, 'Well, I've been wanting to talk to you. Why haven't I been moved back to Mrs Hatfield's tutor group? I recall a definite promise from you last year, and I've been extremely good, and I'm sure you're aware that I am at a very vulnerable age when it comes to friends – this could be detrimental to my self-esteem.'

Unlike my dad, Ramsbottom isn't easily confused by a stream of fast talking. She just held up a hand and waited for me to stop.

'We'll discuss your tutor group in a moment. I think there's the more pressing matter of your treatment of other students.'

What the actual monkey was she talking about? 'But other students love me!' I said.

'No one loves being placed in danger.'

'I don't follow.'

She scowled. 'We discussed your disregard for safety last term.'

'I'm afraid I'm still not with you, Miss Ramsbottom. Perhaps you could act it out, like in a game of charades?'

'Faith! I don't think you should make light of attempting to throw another girl down the stairs!'

Oh please. It's a wonder Miss Ramsbottom manages day-to-day life. She gets the wrong end of the stick so badly that she doesn't even know what is stick and what's not. It seems like a miracle to me that she's never been arrested for falsely accusing someone of murder.

I said, 'Is this about Angharad? I was just steadying her while she leant over the banisters to take in the stimulating sight of three hundred girls hurrying to their education.'

'Mr Hampton said that you were about to toss her down the stairs.'

Which is funny because you wouldn't expect a man who wears as much corduroy as Mr Hampton to over exaggerate like that. I didn't mention this because Miss Ramsbottom gets very twitchy when I make remarks about other teachers. I just said, 'She liked it.'

'That seems highly unlikely.'

'You've got to take into account Angharad's extreme titchiness. She just wanted to see what it was like to look down from a great height.'

'Whether the girl in question gave her consent or not, I would have thought that you could have recognised what an inappropriate, not to mention dangerous, action it was.'

I bowed my head because I find these little chats move along quicker if I pretend to be sorry.

'What if you had dropped her?'

We had, of course, taken the precaution of tying the belt from Megs's coat round Ang and to the stair rail. Does she think I'm an idiot? But, along with the head bowing, total silence helps Miss R get it out of her system much faster, so I kept my lips pressed together.

'She could have been seriously injured. I expect more sense from a Year Ten.'

Does that mean that she wouldn't mind if Year Sevens started flinging people down the stairs?

'You'll be in Year Ten detention next week. I'll speak to the other young lady in question. What's her name?'

See? She doesn't listen to a word I say. I was tempted to claim it was Icky Blundell, but using her name didn't work out too well for me last term, so I said, 'Angharad Jones.'

Eventually, she seemed to run out of lecture

power and was about to dismiss me, but I said, 'What about me moving back to Mrs Hatfield's tutor group? Remember you promised last term?'

She flared her nostrils at me. 'I remember no such thing. You were moved to a different tutor group because you seemed unable to concentrate when you were in a class with Megan.'

'It's true that Megs can be very distracting, but last term—'

'I said that we would review the situation. I have reviewed it. Despite the slight improvement in your conduct, I think that today's incident demonstrates admirably why you won't be moving back to Mrs Hatfield's form this term.'

I may have puffed out my breath in a quiet, non-aggressive sort of way.

'There's no need for that sort of thing. Faith, this is about your choices. You're old enough to know what the right thing to do is.'

Honestly, it's a wonder that she doesn't bore herself to death sometimes. It's probably the reason she's so pale.

In the end she let me go and I arrived late to Maths. Maths (and English and Science) are taught in sets and Megs and I are both clever, so actually I still sit next to her for these lessons. I'm not sure that Miss Ramsbottom has realised. It would be quite funny to point this out to her, but Mum taught me not to wind up people who are stupider than me, so I haven't bothered.

Mrs Baxter was already doing one of her long rambly explanations. I sat down and Megs whispered, 'What happened?'

'Detention.'

She shook her head.

'And Ramsbum says I can't come back to Mrs Mad-as-a-Hatfield's tutor group.'

'No way!'

I nodded sadly.

Mrs B interrupted to tell us to do exercise nine.

'I can't believe it!' Megs whispered.

'It's extremely tragic. I hardly get a minute with you these days.' I flicked open the textbook and said, 'Now let's spend the next hour talking about my birthday plans.'

WEDNESDAY 11TH JANUARY

I'm depressed about Ramsbottom going back on her word and not letting me return to my original tutor group with Megs. When I got to registration this morning, I said, 'Have you heard the news, Mrs Webber? I'm stuck with you lot.'

Mrs Webber didn't even stop marking books. She just smiled and said, 'Well, with a positive attitude like that, I'm sure that we'll all get along swimmingly.'

I sighed. 'Have some sympathy, Mrs W. You know what it's like when you dangle a tiny girl over the banisters and some old vampire in heels gets all uptight about it and won't let you hang out with your best mate.'

Mrs W gave me a long look. Eventually, she said, 'Let's just say I appreciate your disappointment.'

LATER

Because my mum is always asking me to share my news with her, I thought I'd tell her about my birthday plans. In fact, I gave her a folder containing a guest list, venue suggestions and a first draft of the menu.

She folded her arms and said, 'We can't afford to hire anywhere for your birthday, Faith.'

I'm used to this kind of negativity every time I try to follow my dreams, so I said, 'I suppose we could have it here. We'll just have to take out most of the furniture to fit everybody in.'

'No. We're not having it here either. Not after last year.'

'When are you going to stop going on about that? We fixed the ceiling, Neesha's hair grew back and Sam didn't need therapy after all, did he?'

We both turned to look at Sam who was adding

more blood to his painting of an explosion in a pet shop.

'At least not for that anyway.'

Mum sighed. 'The point is I don't think we can trust you to have another party for quite some time.'

'What about a really small one? Just fifty or sixty of my closest friends?'

'No.'

'What if I'm really good between now and my birthday?'

'I'm not going to give in on this one, Faith. You're not having a birthday party.'

I drooped.

'I tell you what, if you are angelic between now and the summer holidays, maybe you'll be allowed a small gathering. That means good reports from school and keeping your room tidy.'

So no party for me.

I wonder how many people I could fit in the shed.

THURSDAY 12TH JANUARY

Finn has finally got in touch. I was all happy when his name came up on my phone because I assumed he wanted to meet up, but no; instead, he sent me a picture of a monkey. No message. Just a monkey in a baseball cap.

I've checked all my magazines and none of them have any suggestions as to what this means. I was expecting another date. I got a monkey.

It's nice that he's keeping in touch, but seriously. A monkey.

LATER
A pigging monkey.

LATER STILL
I hate monkeys.

FRIDAY 13TH JANUARY
On the way to school I asked Megs if Cameron ever sends her random pictures of animals wearing hats.

She shook her head. 'No, but he does keep me up to date on any important football player transfers.'

'And you like that?'

'Well, I'm glad that he's sharing his big news with me.'

'I'm really not sure that I can muster enthusiasm for anyone's monkey news.'

'It's just a friendly text. Think of it as like a smiley face.'

'I suppose the monkey was grinning in a toothy, creepy, I'm-going-to-eat-your-face sort of way.'

Megs shook her head at me. 'You're the only person I know that doesn't like cute pictures of animals.'

'There you go, Megs, you've finally proved my theory that I am the sole sane voice in your nutty existence.'

Anyway, I can deal with a few chimps if another date is on its way.

When I got to registration, the first thing Lily said was, 'It's Friday the thirteenth.'

Mrs Webber said, 'That's superstitious nonsense.'

'A lot of bad things have happened on Friday the thirteenth,' Lily said and she glanced up at the ceiling as if she was expecting lightning to strike. 'It's a day when evil forces abound and there's wickedness in the air.'

Mrs Webber looked at Lily. 'Just another day at Westfield High then.'

At lunchtime Icky came up to me in the canteen. 'I had a really good chat with Finn last night. He's so friendly, isn't he? He couldn't stop hugging me.'

Obviously, I was wondering what on earth Finn was doing in the same place as Icky, but I was determined not to get upset. Icky thinks that if a boy sneezes in her direction it's a declaration of love. So I just said, 'It's nice he took pity on you.

When we were on one of our dates, he did say he was thinking about doing some charity work.'

'Yeah, right, like you two went on a date!'

'They did,' Megs said. 'They've been on loads.'

'Next time he's cuddling up to me, I'll ask him about that.'

And she smarmed off.

My mum always says that you should just let nasty people get it out of their system and not get into a slanging match.

Where's the fun in that?

So I shouted after her, 'Vicky! Today is Friday the thirteenth!'

She turned back to give me a withering look. 'I know what the date is.'

'Really? I just assumed that you'd got it confused with Halloween since you're wearing that terrifying mask.'

I had the double satisfaction of Icky going purple and most of the canteen falling about laughing.

The rest of the day was filled with that annoying education stuff. I forget what they were cramming our heads with today.

Just before the bell went for home time, I said to Lily, 'Nothing Friday the thirteenthish happened in the end, did it?'

Lily pulled her spooky face and, just at that

moment, Angharad flung herself off the desk behind Lily and jumped on her back.

Lily went, 'Ah! Ah! Ahhhhh! What the hell, Angharad? I thought you were an evil spirit!'

And I nearly died laughing.

Angharad was snorting so hard that she couldn't climb down from leggy Lily's back properly. She just slid down her into a puddle on the floor and Lily jabbed her in the stomach with her boot. It was comedy at its finest.

SATURDAY 14TH JANUARY

This morning I texted Granny and asked her if she thought that girls should ask boys out. She replied, **Modern, intelligent ones that know what they want should.**

Obviously, any idiot knows that I'm modern and intelligent and I definitely know what I want. In fact, usually, I'm really quite good at expressing my wants and needs (for instance, just now I poked my head out from under the duvet and yelled, 'Can we have pizza for lunch?' down the stairs). So I should take Granny's advice and ask Finn on a date. I suppose that I've been holding back because I sort of want to know that he wants to before I ask.

But you can't always know what other people want. For example, who could have known that

Miss Ramsbottom would object to that sing-song I started in the corridor outside her office yesterday?

I'll just have to go for it. I'm definitely going to text him.

Might just spend a few minutes thinking about what to say.

LATER
I've almost finished composing my text. Just need to ring a few people to see what they think.

LATER AGAIN
Got distracted on the phone to Megs and started talking about Icky. Megs said it was true that she did talk to Finn in McDonald's the other night, but no one saw any actual hugging. Anyway, Icky is now dating someone called Kieran who is apparently her third boyfriend this year. I bet she doesn't faff about when it comes to texting boys. I'm sending a text asking Finn to the park tomorrow, right now.

THIRTY SECONDS LATER
He hasn't replied. Why not?

FIVE MINUTES LATER
I have had enough of this. I'm going to Megs's house to get my second dose of pizza.

MUCH LATER

Woo! When I was walking back from Megs's, Finn texted to say yes. There was also a picture of a monkey doing the thumbs-up sign.

As you know, I have always liked monkeys.

SUNDAY 15TH JANUARY

I love going on dates with Finn, but I can't help thinking that I might enjoy it more if we lived in a huge house and there was a poolroom where we could hang out. There aren't many places in town that you can go to for cheap. We started at Juicy Lucy's, but I only had enough money for a milkshake, so after a bit Finn said, 'Let's go for a walk.'

I'm not normally a big fan of walking; it's like being polite and not slouching: I do enough of it at school. Of course, I have suggested many times that we should get those little golf carts to transport us between lessons, but you know how Ramsbottom feels about my marvellous ideas. Anyway, I have discovered that walking with Finn is much more rewarding. Mostly because we can walk to places where no one is staring and then there is kissing.

We walked down to the river. It was completely freezing, but I had a happy glow to keep me warm.

Finn asked me if I'd got any brothers and sisters.

'Not in the traditional sense,' I said, 'but there is this creepy, worm-like creature that hangs around our house, begging for scraps.'

Finn's eyes widened. 'What? Like a snake?'

'Yeah, a lot like a snake.'

'Wait a minute; didn't I see you with a kid in the supermarket?'

I was hoping that he'd forgotten about that. I had peas in my hair at the time.

'I've got a little brother called Sam,' I admitted.

'And he's the snake! You're funny, Faith.'

I tried to look modest.

'What about you?' I asked. 'Who's in your family?'

'Mum and Dad. My bro.'

'Is he like a snake?'

'No! He's more like a ... what kind of animal has got long hair?'

'A Shetland pony? A sheepdog?'

'Yeah, a sheepdog. A friendly one. Noah's cool.'

I can't imagine describing any of my family as 'cool'. Unless, of course, I'd whacked them over the head and then hidden them in the freezer. But Finn explained that he and his older brother get on really well. They also seem to like their parents. Imagine all that family harmony.

I said, 'I would get on with my family if they weren't all such idiots.'

Finn laughed again, but I wasn't joking.

There was no one else walking by the river and after a bit we sat down on a bench. It was icy and on the other side of the river we could see frosty fields that looked like they'd been dusted with icing sugar. It was very pretty. Even lovelier was when Finn put his arm round me. I had a great time and when we said goodbye Finn said, 'See you soon.' Which is definite progress.

MONDAY 16TH JANUARY

They're always going on about how school prepares us for adult life. I don't know any adults who are expected to do chemical equations and then lollop around the hockey field on the same day. Old people are punishing us for being young and good-looking.

TUESDAY 17TH JANUARY

At break time we tucked up in the PE equipment cupboard to avoid the icy breezes outside and also the icy breezes inside wherever Miss Ramsbottom is. Everyone was looking a bit droopy. January is not a cheerful month.

'I miss choir,' Ang said.

I never thought I'd miss anything that involved Mr Millet, but it's true that things are not quite the same this term. We're lacking a certain something and I think that that something might be a once-a-week encounter with a herd of boys.

'I don't see why choir had to end,' Megs said.

'I heard that some of the Year Elevens went to ask Mr Millet if we could carry on this term,' Lily said.

I sat up. 'What did he say?'

'He said that he's got too much work to do with the orchestra this term to commit to another extra-curricular club.'

Angharad nodded. 'That's understandable.'

Lily was attempting the splits on top of a pommel horse. 'He also said that he was never organising another activity that allowed overly hormonal teenagers in the same room.'

'What a cheek! Did he really say that?' I asked.

'Yep,' said Megs, who I'm pretty sure knew nothing about the whole thing. 'He said he'd had enough of snog-crazy teens. Especially ginger ones.'

I gave her a flying kick.

Angharad rolled out of the way of our wrestling and said, 'But I do miss choir. It was nice to see ... people.'

'You saw Elliot last Sunday.'

'I know, but it's not a regular thing like choir.'

She had a point there. I'd probably see more of Finn if we did a club together every week.

Angharad sighed. 'I wish Elliot and I were official like Megs and Cam, or semi-official like you and Finn.'

I took a moment to pity Ang and Lily and their lack of almost-boyfriends. Angharad seemed to appreciate my sympathetic look, but Lily was busy balancing a football on her nose.

'It'd be good if we could think of another way of gathering the boys and girls together again,' Megs said.

Everyone looked at me because they can't come up with their own ideas. Unfortunately, I couldn't think of my own idea either, so I just stared back at them.

'Something like the Christmas boxes,' Lily said.

Ang nodded her head. 'Yes, that was fun, wasn't it, Faith?'

'Maybe for you. When you're the woman in charge, it's all stress, stress, stress.'

'But you were really good at it, Faith,' Megs said, pulling her sucking-up face, which is the same as the face she does when I yank hairs out of her arm.

'Couldn't you think of another charity thing for us to do?' Ang asked.

'Don't be ridiculous,' I said. 'Nobody expects you to do more than one charitable thing in your life.' I looked at their hopeful little faces. 'Do they?'

Actually, I might consider doing the boxes again. When we delivered them, the old people's wrinkly faces lit up like their flammable polyester cardies had caught on fire. I used to think that old people were sharp-tongued and bitter, but you can't blame me for that; I only had Granny to go on.

I promised the girls that I would apply my brilliant mind to the important issue of how to get us a guaranteed weekly date with the boys again.

LATER

This evening I thought that perhaps I'd give my dad an opportunity to do something to justify his existence.

I said, 'Dad, I need you to think about something for me.'

He put his boring book down. 'Of course, always happy to share my wisdom.'

'Yeah, well, I've already asked all the intelligent people I know so I'm left with you and Mum.'

'I see. What is it that you want me to apply my dim wits to?'

'When you were young, which I appreciate is a long time ago, but when you were at school – they did have schools in those days, didn't they?' He rolled his eyes and I said, 'Is that a yes or a no? As

Miss Ramsbottom likes to shout in my ear, sarcasm is not the answer.'

He nodded his head. And carried on rolling his eyes at the same time.

'Ew, don't do that! It makes you look like that time at Auntie Joyce's wedding when you had too much wine and fell asleep in your chair with your head lolling backwards.'

'Are we getting any closer to the question, Faith? Only I do have to go to bed in three hours' time.'

'Did your school ever do stuff with a girls' school?'

'We *were* a girls' school.'

I nearly fell off the arm of the sofa. 'You went to a girls' school? That explains *a lot*.'

'That's not quite what I meant. It was a girls' school and a boys' school. Mixed sex.'

I had to sit down and help myself to the emergency KitKat that I keep under the sofa. 'You went to a mixed school? Why am I not at a mixed-sex school?'

Dad laughed. And laughed. And laughed. 'I may be a dimwit,' he said, 'but even I know that you at a school with boys is a bad idea.'

So I didn't bother asking him for any suggestions. He didn't need to find ways to spend time with the opposite sex when he was a lad back in Victorian times. Mind you, the girls at his school must have been a fairly ropy lot for him to be so impressed by Mum.

WEDNESDAY 18TH JANUARY

It was Art today. I quite enjoy Art. The important thing is to remember that art is subjective. That means that no one can ever tell you that your work is rubbish. They don't have to like it, but they can't say that it's rubbish because art means different things to different people.

While we were drawing animals, Ang peered over my shoulder. 'Oh, that's really good,' she said.

Although art is subjective and no one can tell you you're rubbish, I firmly believe in taking compliments where you can find them so I didn't argue with Ang. In fact, I was feeling quite chuffed until she peered at Lily's work and said, 'That's really good too.'

I don't care what anyone says about art meaning different things to different people. I'm pretty sure that everyone could agree that Lily's work was not good. I suppose I should make allowances for Ang since she mostly lives out her life between the covers of a Maths textbook and is a bit dazzled by bright colours. There were certainly a lot of bright colours in Lily's work. She held it up and squinted at it. 'Does it look like a horse?'

Because I was practising something Megs suggested about not saying what I really think all the time, I said, 'Oh yes. Totally looks like a horse.'

Lily put down her coloured pencil. 'It's not a very good cow then, is it?'

But Lily is never worried about things like this. She just added a saddle and what looked like a kitten riding it.

'Is that me?' Ang asked, pointing to the kitten thing.

Lily looked from the kitten to Angharad and back again. 'Mmm-hmm,' she said, rubbing out the whiskers and adding a ponytail. 'Definitely you.'

'That's brilliant.' Angharad beamed. 'They should put that up. They should put it in one of those display cases by reception. You know, the ones that lock.'

'They should put something in a locked case,' I said, looking at Lily who was now painting her knees.

THURSDAY 19TH JANUARY

I haven't got any further with my plans to bring the boys' school the delight of spending time with us lot, so I was forced to consult Mum.

While she was washing up and I was helping by eating things left on the plates, I said, 'Did you go to a mixed-sex school?'

Mum smiled. 'No.'

'Why not?'

'Granny said she wanted me to learn something useful like typing or cooking. She thought that if I was around boys I'd waste time twirling my hair and flashing my knickers.'

Granny had a point there. I remember that time Mum did a cartwheel on the beach. No one should have to see what's under her skirt. But even taking that into account it was a rubbish approach to your daughter's education.

'Sounds sexist to me and she obviously failed with the cooking,' I said, licking the apple crumble dish. 'What was the typing about? Did she want you to go into ICT?'

'No, she wanted me to be a typist.'

I stopped mid-lick. 'People aren't wrong when they say that things were simpler in the olden days, are they? Imagine typing being a whole job. I could do that with one hand.'

'You should be grateful that I've got higher hopes for you.'

'Higher? What, like a trapeze artist?'

'I was thinking more of something sciencey.'

I gave her a stern look. 'Something *sciencey*? Well, that won't be happening if I've inherited your standards of precision, will it? Sciencey isn't even a word, let alone a job description.'

She got a bit bristly about that. 'It's not my field. Maybe you wouldn't be any good at Social Anthropology.'

'I could be if I wanted to, but you're right: I think I'll do a proper subject at university. Probably Chemistry.'

I don't know why, but that made her purse her lips. 'If you've finished pointing out the holes in my education then maybe I could answer your original question.'

I nodded graciously because I may marry into the royal family and I am practising the moves.

'We did sometimes meet up with the boys' school,' Mum said.

I nodded again.

'There was the school musical.'

I shook my head. 'The problem with musicals is that not everyone seems to appreciate the unique quality of my voice.'

'You don't have to have a main part. You could always just be in the chorus ...' She looked at me. 'No, wait a minute; I've just remembered who I'm talking to. You're not going to be happy in the background, are you?'

'I'm not good at blending in. I think it's my hair.'

'I think it's your mouth.'

'Have you got any other suggestions? Or shall

I be off to look up that care home I'm going to put you in when you're older?'

'What care home?'

'That one we saw the documentary on, where they spit in your soup.'

Mum narrowed her eyes. 'Actually, I've got several more suggestions. When you've made your poor old mother a cup of herbal tea, I'll tell you.'

So I made her a cup of her bark and moss tea without even swearing, although I must say that it's disgusting the way parents bribe their children these days. I bet princesses don't have to make their ancient mothers cups of tea.

Once she was settled with the fruits of my labour, she said, 'You could do some charity work—'

'*Urgh*, no more talk of charity. It's sucking the life out of me.'

'All right, you could organise a litter pick.'

'Oh, come on! Is it not possible to spend time in the company of boys and do something enjoyable at the same time? Or are you worried that the double fun would kill me because I've never experienced it before in my sad little life?'

'Life is what you make it, my petal. If you bring sunshine, you get sunshine.'

I wondered what the royals do when someone is annoying them. Maybe call for the executioner?

Mum was looking at me.

'What? Is it illegal to even think about chopping your family's heads off now?'

Mum huffed. 'I've thought of a kind of club that you'd enjoy.'

'Go on.'

'When I was at college, I was a member of the debating society. Oh, we had a really good time.'

'Sounds riveting,' I said, but she carried on in that selfish way of hers.

'I can still remember the two debates that I won. The first one was about animal testing and the other was about nuclear power. Kids used to be really interested in the environment in those days.'

I nodded like the queen does when she's forced to listen to some idiot. 'So you did this debating with boys?'

'That wasn't actually the sole purpose of the society, but yes, I remember there were several boys. In fact, I dated one of them.' A look came over her face like Lily eyeing a peanut butter and marmite sandwich. Gross. 'I remember this one time we were in the canteen and he leant over and—'

'Please, Mum! I still haven't managed to erase the memory of you and Dad holding hands at the cinema that time; I don't have the mental energy to block out any more toxic images.'

'All right, all right! I'll say no more about his lovely full lips.'

'Mum!'

'Or the fact that he knew how to use them.'

'Mother!'

'He used to turn me to jelly.'

I stuck my fingers in my ears and started singing the hokey-cokey.

Mum fanned herself then pulled my hands down. 'Do you want to hear about debating then?'

'Yes,' I said, but I was unable to nod regally because I still felt queasy.

'It's quite easy to set up a debating club. You just need someone to organise things. We had a different debate each week. Usually, you have a proposer of the motion and a seconder. Perhaps you could do boys against girls.'

I thought about this. 'Debating is basically arguing, isn't it?'

Mum nodded.

'I think we've found something I can shine at.'

'Good. Now do you think you could wipe the table?'

But I was already off up the stairs giving her a royal wave.

FRIDAY 20TH JANUARY

Finally, Finn has sent me a text. It says, **Football**

on Sun? Which I assume means he wants me to go and watch him play football.

I rang Megs.

Eventually, she picked up her phone and said, 'What do you want?'

'There she is! My sunshine in the dark winter months.'

'Oh God, you *do* want something, don't you?'

'You're going to watch Cam play football on Sunday.'

'Don't you mean, "*Are* you going to watch Cam?" ?'

'No, I mean you are. You have to because Finn has asked me to watch him.'

'Oh well, if you need me to hang about because it's convenient for you then obviously I'll drop everything. It's not like I've got my own mind, or my own interests, or even a voice to speak up about what I want. I'm just here to please you. You may as well write me a timetable.'

'I'll do that. In the mean time I'll meet you by the swings at nine.'

She hung up.

Which I took as a yes.

LATER

That Megs has got a cheek. I've just remembered that time I dragged myself out of my comfy bed in the early hours to go and hang about the frozen football pitch and support her with her Cam-love. I wanted to say this to her in a text, but I couldn't be bothered to type it all so I just put, **I did it for you!**

Two minutes later she said, **Oh, all right. You'd better bring me some sweeties.**

SATURDAY 21ST JANUARY

Granny came round for lunch. I said, 'Have you not got anything to eat at your house, Granny? That's because you're always out having a good time with your boyfriends. You ought to concentrate on your shopping and your knitting like a proper old lady.'

Granny gave me a smile like a crocodile about to snap the head off a baby frog. 'When I actually get old, I might give that some thought.'

I don't believe a word of it. She'll be winking at the pall-bearers when she's in her coffin.

'And what are you concentrating on at the moment, Faith?' Granny asked. 'I hope you've made a New Year's resolution to work hard at school.'

'I don't make resolutions. You're always telling me not to make promises I can't keep. Anyway, I don't think I should start trying to improve on my almost-perfection. If I became totally perfect then people would find it hard to root for me when I'm warring with teachers.'

'I've made lots of resolutions,' Granny said, turning to Sam, which is her way of letting me know that she doesn't think I'm doing the conversation the right way.

Sam didn't look up from his terrible drawing of a skeleton army. 'What resolutions, Granny?' he asked.

'I've decided to try something new every week. I've signed up for three evening classes and I'm going to be more adventurous with what I eat.' She looked round at us, waiting for us to be impressed or excited or something.

She was lucky I was still awake.

I think my resolution is to spend less time with my family.

SUNDAY 22ND JANUARY

Football was surprisingly good fun. If you've got to watch sport then it helps if your boyfriend happens to be the fittest player on the pitch, in both senses of the word. Afterwards, we all went for hot chocolate, which reminded me of Finn: sweet, warm and delicious.

I could tell that Megs was making an effort to chat to Finn. She's not a bad banana sometimes. Cam and Finn mostly talked about football, with a little bit of surfing and skateboarding thrown in. Their whole conversation was a bit too much like an activity holiday and I had to eat half of Megs's cookie to keep my strength up. When Finn was getting another drink, I asked Cam what he thought of Finn.

'He's an old-fashioned centre half: strong in the tackle and a sweet left foot. I haven't seen him surf, but I've heard he's really good.'

'Mmm,' I said. 'That's a pretty thorough PE report, but really I was wondering what you thought of him as a person.'

Cam shrugged. 'Yeah, he's all right.'

Which I took to mean that Cam thinks Finn is as brilliant as I do. I don't know why Ethan doesn't like him.

And we've arranged another date. We're meeting up on Thursday.

MONDAY 23RD JANUARY

I told the girls about my brilliant plan for an inter-school debating club. You know when you assume that people are as intelligent as you are and that they will receive your obviously genius idea with the cheering and hugs that it deserves? Well, I never assume that with my lot because they're all idiots. Which is why Megs pulled a face and Ang said, 'Oh.' And Lily tried to look at the label inside the neck of her jumper while she was still wearing it. (Although, to be fair to Lily, she had been doing that for several minutes before I even suggested the debating club.)

'Thanks for your support,' I said.

'Just a minute,' Megs said. 'Let me get this straight; you want us to have shouting matches with the boys? Is that a good way to impress them?'

'Megan! If a boy only likes me if I agree with him then I am not interested in him.'

Angharad nodded vigorously. Lily nodded as vigorously as she could while her head was stuck half in and half out of her jumper.

'I mean, anyone is welcome to adore me from afar,' I said. 'But that's as far as it goes. I couldn't possibly date someone who didn't respect my opinions.'

'You normally just beat up people who don't agree with you,' Megs said.

'And have you learnt nothing from that? We all need to be firm in our beliefs.'

Then Lily chipped in. 'My mum says we should all be ourselves. That's the only way to find someone who is perfect for you. There's a lid for every pot. That's what she says.'

There was a moment of silence while we all contemplated exactly what kind of crazy boy-lid would match Lily's potty pot.

'Actually,' said Megs, 'I am quite myself with

Cam ... just not the myself that eats tuna straight from the can or picks her toenails.'

'I think that counts as good manners rather than hiding your inner light,' I said. 'Anyway, now that we're all clear that we'll never be the kind of girl that just agrees with a boy for the sake of it, can we get back to my brilliant idea?'

Megs sniffed. 'I thought you told me earlier that it was your mum's idea.'

'She's my mum; she's supposed to give me all her good stuff.'

'I'm not sure about this debating,' Megs said. 'Don't you think that the boys will have an unfair advantage because they've got foghorn Westy?'

'It's not about who argues the loudest. It's about who argues the bestest and who is most, you know, good with words.'

'Do we have to speak in front of everyone?' Angharad asked.

I smiled at her. 'Yep. It'll be good for you, Ang. After a couple of weeks' practice, you'll be talking at levels audible to all, instead of just those who have got their ear pressed against your lips.'

'I know someone who'd like to press their ear to Ang's lips,' Lily said.

'Oooh, yes!' I patted Ang enthusiastically on the back. 'Have you got any further with Elliot?'

'We have had a couple of conversations by text.'

'And?' I asked. 'What's happening?'

Angharad adopted an expression of great dignity and said, 'We're taking it slowly.'

'That's amazing!' Megs gushed.

I was starting to feel jealous. 'So you actually had a chat about your relationship, did you?'

'Well, not exactly,' Ang said. 'We're going so slowly that we haven't quite got to the conversation about taking it slowly yet.'

It was pretty easy to convince Ang that she and Elliot definitely need the debating club to help them along, but I spent the rest of the day persuading Megs and Lily. I think they're coming round to the idea, but it's left me exhausted.

I hope convincing the teachers requires less punching.

TUESDAY 24TH JANUARY

A poster has gone up at school for a club night next month.

'What's a club night?' Lily asked. 'Is it like Brownies?'

We looked at the poster. 'I think it's meant to be like a nightclub,' Megs said. 'You know, music and dancing and people posing.'

'What here? In the school hall?' Angharad asked.

'You're right,' I said. 'It probably will be more like Brownies.'

The poster said the club night has been organised by Year Eleven as part of their charity fund-raising.

'Zoe says that Icky is on the fund-raising committee,' Angharad said.

My mouth fell open. 'How does she do it?' I asked.

'Do what?' Ang asked.

'She always manages to get into everything. Committees, Year Eleven cliques, boys' mouths ...'

'I'm not sure this club night is going to be anything to be proud of,' Megs said. 'Who wants to go to a party at school?'

'Bet the music will be awful,' Angharad said.

Lily screwed up her face. 'They'll have teachers on patrol to stop any snogging.'

'We're really too cool to even bother turning up,' Megs said.

We all nodded.

'Which just leaves us with one question,' I said. 'What are we going to wear?'

LATER

To help Ang along with Elliot while we're getting the debating club off the ground, Megs has arranged for us to meet the boys in the park on

Saturday. I wasn't sure about going when Megs first suggested it.

I said to her, 'You shouldn't just assume that I'm free. What if I was meeting Finn?'

She pursed her lips. 'Are you meeting Finn?'

'Not at the moment.'

'You can't hang about like a lemon waiting for him to call. You're coming out with us.'

I let her bully me, just this once. 'I can see that you're on the verge of tears because you can't bear the thought of being away from me so I'll come.'

'Good, you'll enjoy seeing Ethan,' Megs smirked.

'I'll enjoy seeing *everyone*.'

WEDNESDAY 25TH JANUARY

When I got to school this morning, I couldn't find my registration snack or my Chemistry homework, so I emptied the contents of my bag on the table. I still couldn't find my post-breakfast pasty, but I did find a couple of Bourbons that were only a bit fluffy around the edges. While I was tucking in, Mrs Webber arrived. I thought I'd let her in on my brilliant idea about debating.

I said, 'Mrs W, I am going to set up a club. It's completely educational and will keep us off the streets and all that. I know how you love to support young people with their futures as long as it doesn't interfere with your online poker playing, so when you've got a minute free could you sort the room out for me? Something with a coffee machine would be good.'

Mrs Webber held up a hand. 'Hold on, hold on, what's this all about, Faith?'

'I want to start a debating club with the boys' school.'

'I see.' She curled her lip up in that quite annoying way she has. You'd think, when she was younger, that she would have slept with her mouth Sellotaped into a more attractive arrangement to sort that out.

'You've got such a suspicious nature, Mrs W!' I said. 'It's all above board. Just a select handful of gifted and talented boys and girls learning the ancient art of arguing. That's pretty wholesome, isn't it?'

She unbuttoned her lip to say, 'It will need organising.'

'I can organise.'

Mrs Webber looked pointedly at the contents of my bag which were still higgledy-piggledy on the table.

I fished out my Chemistry book from the sweet wrappers and misdemeanour slips. 'See? This is exactly where I thought it would be.'

Mrs W leant forward and peeled off the remains of a marmite sandwich from the front cover.

I puffed out a breath of exasperation. 'Well, I'm not going to be organising sandwiches, am I?'

'I think you'll find that teenagers require a lot more instruction than bread products.'

'What? Honestly, you adults make such a fuss about looking after teenagers. All we really need is large amounts of cash and food.'

'And someone to mop up afterwards.' Mrs Webber helped herself to one of the Skittles in my bag pile. 'I admire your commitment to extra-curricular activities, Faith, but you'll have to find a teacher to help you run it. Why don't you try the English department?'

'Because they're a load of self-obsessed, unpublished poets with questionable taste in shoes?'

'Or you could talk to Miss Ramsbottom.'

As you know, I have always been very fond of the English department.

THURSDAY 26TH JANUARY

I met Finn in Juicy Lucy's after school. I'd been thinking about what I said to the girls about how you have to be firm in your beliefs when talking to boys, so I decided that I should discuss my firmest belief with Finn – the one where I believe that Finn should be my boyfriend. After a bit of preliminary chit-chat about whether Spider-Man would be any good at surfing, I said, 'So ... we've been seeing each other a bit.'

Finn nodded.

'I have a good time with you.'

'I have a good time with you too, Faith. You're always telling funny stories.'

'Oh, thanks.'

'Like the crazy vampire lady story you made up.'

I didn't think it was the time to explain that while Miss Ramsbottom seems to be the stuff of horror films she is actually terrifyingly real, so I moved on.

'Um ...' Which wasn't the opening I'd rehearsed in my head. 'I was thinking that maybe we should make it official.'

'Official?' His nose creased like he was afraid there was paperwork involved.

'You know, like boyfriend and girlfriend.'

For a split second, I thought he was going to tell me that he was a free spirit and didn't want to be tied down, but instead his face cracked into a smile and he said, 'That would be awesome.'

Which is pretty ... awesome.

So it's official. Finn Ryland is my boyfriend.

FRIDAY 27TH JANUARY
I don't want to become one of those types who

only talks about their extremely attractive, adorable and sweet boyfriend, so I thought I'd bless my friends with some help with their own love lives. As you know, I am always sensitive in the delicate matter of love, so at lunchtime I said, 'Ang, will it be tongues for you and Elliot at the park tomorrow?'

Ang looked like I'd given her an electric shock.

'No? Maybe you could just warm up with a bit of direct eye contact?'

Ang nodded and squared her shoulders in the way that soldiers do before they march off to war. 'I've got a few topics of conversation planned,' she said. 'I thought I'd start by asking how the cold weather affects his paper round.'

'Uh-huh, sounds like a cosy time for you two. What about you, Lily? How about getting snoggy with Westy?'

Lily drew herself up tall and looked down her nose at us. 'I'm afraid my affections are engaged elsewhere.'

We laughed our heads off.

'Yeah,' said Lily, slouching again. 'But I *am* sort of seeing someone.' She went back to picking the raisins out of her muffin.

Megs and I squealed, 'WHAT?'

Angharad, I noticed, said nothing. 'You knew!' I said to her. 'I will sit on you as soon as

I don't need all my attention on interrogating Lily.'

'Who is it?' Megs said. 'What's happening? Is he your boyfriend? Or just sort of, you know? Where did you meet him?'

I put my hand over her mouth. 'Megan, silence!'

We all looked at Lily.

She smiled. 'It's Arif.'

'Oh,' I said.

Arif is Lily's pen pal. When we were in Year Eight, we had a student teacher who matched us up with pen pals at another school where her friend was studenting. Mine was called Ashley-Rose. She only wrote to me twice. But Lily has been emailing Arif ever since.

'Arif?' Megs said.

Lily nodded.

'Arif that sent you a list of his top one hundred *Star Wars* moments?'

Lily nodded again.

'Arif?'

'Yes, Megs, Arif is the object of Lily's affections,' I said, in order to stop us going round in circles.

Megs pulled a face. 'But ... you two just talk about weird stuff.'

We've all seen Arif's emails. They are mostly

about space travel and characters from sci-fi programmes that the rest of us have never even heard of.

'Things have taken a slightly more romantic turn,' Lily said.

I think my eyes bulged. It's hard to imagine someone you heard dressed up like a dalek for Halloween getting romantic.

'Do you even know what he looks like?' Megs asked.

'I've seen photos.' Lily was starting to sound a bit defensive. 'He's got a nice nose.'

Fortunately, the bell rang at that point which was just as well because I could see that Megs was about to say 'Arif?' again.

SATURDAY 28TH JANUARY

It was our trip to the park today. As usual when we plan to do anything outside, it was absolutely freezing. Ice everywhere. I'm not one to let nature dictate what I wear so I pulled on my thickest tights and my new denim skirt.

I skidded my way round to Megs's house to meet up with the girls and we got to the park before the boys. We headed for our usual spot next to the playground. I was ready for a little sit-down, but when you're wearing a miniskirt it's quite hard to get your legs under a picnic table without flashing the crotch of your tights. I was halfway through this delicate procedure (using Angharad's head for support) when I heard someone shouting, 'HELLO, GIRLS!'

Even though I was mid-bench-straddle, I twisted round to watch the unmistakable bulk of Westy heading towards us. He was on a scooter, pumping his leg to build up speed. He launched himself along the frosty path and it was all going smoothly till he stopped looking where he was going to give us a wave. The scooter hit the edge of the path and he somersaulted over a low fence and landed on his back in the kids' sandpit. For a second, I thought he'd knocked himself out, but then he lifted a wobbly arm and gave us a thumbs up.

Good grief. I wish he'd wear a helmet.

All the time.

The rest of the boys appeared through the trees and gave Westy a round of applause. While I was gawping, Ang said to me, 'Can I have my head back?' which made me sit down sharpish and hope that everybody's eyes had been firmly on Westy and that no one had noticed me airing my knicker region.

The lads came over, tripping each other up and insulting each other's intelligence, looks and sporting ability. Westy ploughed through them on his scooter. He shook sand out of his hair like a dog and said, 'Nice pants, Faith.'

I might have to rethink my dislike of trousers.

We sat about chatting for a while and I explained my brilliant idea for the debating club.

'Sounds like English lessons,' Cam said.

'Sounds like a chance for me to make everyone else feel inferior with my razor-sharp wit,' Ethan said. 'You can count me in. As long as it's not on Mondays because I'm usually in detention.' He rubbed his hands together. 'Making whichever teacher put me there feel inferior with my razor-sharp wit.'

'I'm definitely coming, Faith,' Westy said. 'I'm not good at writing stuff down, but I'm really good at talking. And if anyone gets out of hand and starts fighting I can be security.'

I beamed. Apart from Cam, they seemed very enthusiastic.

'What about you, Elliot?' Megs asked, shooting Angharad a look. 'If we get a debating club set up, will you come?'

Elliot froze. 'Um ... I mean ... I don't really like getting up in front of people and doing stuff.'

'It's only a bit of talking,' I said.

Lily gave me a shove. 'Faith would find it harder to shut up for five minutes. Don't worry, Elliot, Angharad's a bit nervous too, aren't you,

Ang? But we all know you're both really clever. You should give it a go. Doesn't matter if you're not as gobby as this lot.'

Angharad and Elliot exchanged a look. I think they were sympathising with each other, but I can't be sure as it's impossible for me to put myself in the place of a quiet person. Even though I'm pretty sure Miss Ramsbottom and my granny would really like to put a quiet person in place of me.

Anyway, hopefully the whole gang will be getting involved in my debating club. Although, I might have to get Megs to work on Cam. I don't mind if she snogs him or wallops him, as long as she gets him there.

It was getting pretty chilly sitting about on the benches, so Westy suggested that we play a game to warm ourselves up.

'What about Colour Run?' he said.

Ethan started laughing. 'We got banned from playing that.'

'What's Colour Run?' I asked. 'And why were you banned from playing it?'

'We used to play it at primary school with Mr Sachs, didn't we, Westy? He'd call out a colour and we had to run and touch something of that colour. Last person to find something was out.'

Westy snorted with laughter.

'What? What happened?' Megs asked.

Ethan smirked. 'One time we were playing and Mr Sachs called out, "Orange!"'

Ethan loves to string a story out so I said, 'Yes? And? Come on!'

'The only orange thing in the room was his tracksuit ...'

Angharad's little eyes stretched wide.

'... He might have been all right if it hadn't been Westy that got to him first.'

Westy gave Ethan a shove. 'It wasn't me that broke his leg!'

'No,' said Ethan. 'It was the thirty other kids who piled in on top of you.'

We had a go at Colour Run for a while. Even though I don't generally approve of being made to run about, it was quite good fun. I don't know why, but we all seemed to enjoy dashing about like a load of little kids. Maybe it was something to do with the fact that the game provided the opportunity to keep crashing into the opposite sex. Angharad was practically swooning after she and Elliot enjoyed several highly-charged elbow bumps.

While we were still in a silly mood, we played Sardines. Whoever was 'it' had to hide and if you found them you had to get into their hiding spot with them so that eventually everybody was squished into the same place like sardines. When it was Ethan's turn to hide, I was the first one to find him in the little playhouse in the playground. I had to crouch to get in the door. He was sitting on the tiny bench.

'Welcome to my place,' he said gesturing round.

'Nice, I like what you've done with it. That empty crisp packet gives it a real shabby chic feel.'

He looked down at the small amount of bench left beside him and then raised his eyebrows at me. It was like he was daring me to sit down.

So I sat down. The whole of my left side was very nearly touching the whole of his right side.

'Of course, eventually I'll have a mansion,' he said. 'But this will do until I've found an elderly millionaire to befriend before he dies in suspicious circumstances.'

'You've clearly thought about this. I don't know why teachers are always saying that young people don't plan for the future.'

'They love telling you you've got to plan, and organise and work hard; they're obsessed with hard work.'

'That's because none of them are smart enough to get what they want by fast talking.'

'True. Personally, I've always been glad I've got a big mouth to make up for my lazy spirit.'

I couldn't help it. I looked at his mouth. He has got a big mouth. A rather nice big mouth. 'Lazy or not, you seem like the kind of person who gets what he wants,' I said.

His smile dropped and he stared right at me. 'Not always.'

My heart was thumping at this point. Which was stupid because he can't have meant anything by it. I ran a hand through my hair.

'You've got a scratch,' he said.

I looked down at my wrist. 'Yeah, Megs ought to cover her nails with boxing gloves when she's playing Colour Run.'

He reached out and very gently ran his finger along the raised red line on the back of my hand.

I swallowed.

He looked at me.

I looked at him.

The door crashed open and Westy came barrelling in.

Ethan had pulled his hand away and folded his arms. 'Alright, Westy?' he asked in a completely calm voice.

Westy beamed. 'Got you! Man, it's cramped in here, isn't it? Faith, you'd better sit on my knee.'

Soon after that Megs and Cam found us and there wasn't enough room for us all in the house so the game didn't last much longer. Which was probably a good thing because I felt a bit funny about Ethan.

On the way home, Megs said, 'How long was it before Westy found you and Ethan?'

I tensed. 'Not long.'

'What did you talk about?'

'You know what Ethan's like; he was being sarky.'

'And?'

'And he may have touched my hand where your talons scratched me.'

'He held your hand!'

'He didn't hold it. He was just pointing out where you'd grievously injured me.'

'So he was tenderly comforting you in your hour of pain?'

'Megan, shut up or I will find some specialist lawyers who sue people for causing injuries with their razor sharp nails and I will give them your name.'

She didn't say anything else, but I know what she's thinking. And she's wrong. We all know what a joker Ethan is. He was just mucking about. And it wasn't a big deal.

SUNDAY 29TH JANUARY

We went to Granny's house. On the way there I got a text that said, **Bring biscuits. Make sure you close the garden gate when you come in**.

She's abusing technology. There should be a website where I can report her.

MONDAY 30TH JANUARY

I popped along to see the head of English today. I used all my persuasive powers to illustrate what an educational and empowering experience the debating club will be for all those involved.

I said, 'It'll be, like, really good.'

Mrs Rainbird seemed unconvinced.

'It will help improve our Speaking and Listening grades.'

That got her attention.

'It's a lovely idea, Faith.'

Why do people always say that things are a 'lovely idea' when they're about to tell you that you can't do something?

'You have to remember that the English teachers have other after-school commitments and most of us have got young children too.'

'All the more reason to get out of the house! It will be a refreshing break for you.'

She wrinkled her nose. 'Hmm. I'll bring it up at our department meeting tomorrow. That's as much as I can promise.'

Which I took as a definite yes.

TUESDAY 31ST JANUARY

Dad thinks I should tidy my room. I think I should be allowed to express my teenage angst through underwear and chocolate wrappers on the floor.

Since we disagree, I told him that we'd have to wait for an independent arbitrator to sort things out.

He said, 'Fine, but when your mother gets home she'll say the same thing as me.'

'I didn't mean Mum! She's not independent; you've got her under some sort of hypnotic spell – I can't think of any other reason why she married you.'

'Let's ask Sam then, shall we?'

'I was thinking more of someone from the United Nations.'

'You'll have to do it eventually, Faith, so you may as well start now.'

'I'll do it later.'

'This kind of laziness won't get you far in life.'

I wanted to throw something at him, but I couldn't be bothered to find anything.

FEBRUARY

WEDNESDAY 1ST FEBRUARY

Mrs Rainbird found me at registration this morning and said, 'Good news, Faith! Mrs Lloyd-Winterson has agreed to run our debating club. She'll see you at lunchtime.'

There were several things wrong with that sentence. For starters, it's *my* debating club. Secondly, nothing should ever involve me having to see anyone at lunchtime, unless it's the cook so that she can take my order.

Mrs Lloyd-Winterson is extremely ancient. Even older than Granny. Let's hope they don't plan to have the club in the library: I'm not sure Lloyd-Winterson's heart could take the stairs.

At lunchtime I scoffed my food down quickly. Megs said, 'Are you just eating chocolate snacks today? That's your second Penguin. Did you eat your sandwiches in Geography again?'

I said, 'I haven't got much time. I've got to skip the filler and get straight to the good stuff. I'll be spending the rest of lunch admiring Lloyd-Winterson's neck creases while I convince her to get this debating thing going, so that you lot get to see some boys.'

Lily said, 'I like meeting people, but I'm only really interested in Arif in a boyfriend way.'

'And I can see Cam any time I like,' Megs said. Which isn't what they said when they were begging me to arrange some fraternising time with the boys. They both sounded extremely ungrateful for my sacrifice. Ang, on the other hand, said, 'Thank you so much, Faith.' And handed me her KitKat.

That's more like it.

Before I'd even got to Mrs Lloyd-Winterson's classroom she came up behind me in the corridor and said, 'Good afternoon, Faith.'

I'm not sure whether I should be flattered or concerned that even the teachers who don't teach me seem to know who I am.

She pointed me into her room and smiled. 'I must say it's pleasing to see an interest in the ancient art of rhetoric.'

I pulled my enthusiastic face.

'Don't wince, dear. With a little hard work, we'll soon have this venture off the ground.'

I wasn't keen on this talk of hard work, but I nodded my head anyway. Teachers love nodding. 'Mrs Lloyd-Winterson, I thought that we should offer this opportunity to as many intellectually-starved young people as possible.'

Mrs L-W raised her eyebrows. 'Were you hoping to enlist from an orphanage?'

'I was thinking more of the boys' school.'

'I see.'

And I could tell by her face that she did.

Sometimes old people fool you into thinking they're not paying attention by looking stupid and talking about how things cost several pence more than they used to, but really, because their lives are so empty and they've got nothing else to focus on, the elderly are surprisingly good at sussing people out. I waited for her to tell me that the whole thing was off.

She laced her fingers together and peered at me over them. 'Faith, I've heard in the staffroom how last year's choir turned into something of a youth club. Apparently, some of the attendees had not the slightest grasp of musical theory.'

I widened my eyes to show my disgust that these musical idiots had the cheek to sneak into choir.

'I will agree to speak to the English department at Radcliffe boys' school if you will agree that the primary function of this club will be to participate in debates. Any socialising must be secondary.'

And as she was saying it I swear there was the teeniest little ghost of a shadow of a hint of a smile on her face.

'Oh yes,' I said. 'It's all about the debating with just the smallest side helping of inter-school friendship.'

'Then we are of one mind.'

I wouldn't say that we're exactly of one mind. I

don't really fancy sharing a mind with anyone who thinks it's acceptable to wear a knitted waistcoat. But Mrs L-W seemed happy so I just nodded again.

I went back to tell the girls that, thanks to me, the debating club is officially on. Then I graciously accepted their thanks and their crisps.

LATER

There's been a lot of nodding today. I'm going to have to spend less time agreeing with people tomorrow or I'll end up needing a neck brace.

THURSDAY 2ND FEBRUARY

I went to Juicy Lucy's after school with Finn. We sat downstairs and after a while we were the only people in there. I must say it was nice to snog in the warm for once.

The only problem was that after a few minutes I needed to burp. You'd think that my stupid body would be able to shut up for a bit so that I could enjoy the romance of Finn snogging my face off in a smoothie shop, but no. There was an unmistakable pressure in my chest; I definitely needed to belch. I pulled back, but Finn's face just followed me. I broke free, but he just lunged in for another go. Things were getting desperate. I was starting to panic. What if I burped mid-kiss? I put my hands on his shoulders and pushed him back. His nose was now about ten centimetres from mine, still not a safe distance to let off a belch-bomb. I ducked under the table and started to rummage about in my bag.

'You all right, Faith?' Finn asked.

'Yep.' I very quietly burped with my hand over my mouth. 'Just needed my phone.' I sat up straight again. Finn was watching me with a frown. It struck me that breaking off from a passionate kiss to check your phone is probably quite bad manners.

'Um, I just ... wanted to show you this picture Westy sent me.'

I showed him Westy's most recent text which was of a cat clinging on to a bald man's head.

Finn laughed. 'That's pretty funny! It's like the cat thinks he's his hair or something!'

I gave a weak giggle.

Fortunately, my bubbling insides settled down and we were able to get back to the snogathon. In fact, we kissed for a really long time. We just kept going. My whole face is actually a bit achy, but it was worth it. I don't think I'll ever have enough of kissing him.

When we finally dragged our lips apart to say goodbye, Finn said, 'See you at football on Sunday?'

And I said, 'I'm not sure what I'm doing. I'll let you know.'

Which surprised me because I thought I

was just going to say yes. But you know how my mouth is, always running away from me. My mouth has got a point though; going to football to admire Finn's legs and strange ability to kick a ball between two posts is fine once in a while, but I don't want to only be known as a footballer's girlfriend. And it would be a mistake for anyone to think that I'm someone who just does what her boyfriend likes all the time.

Because, as you know, I am quite keen on doing things that I like.

FRIDAY 3RD FEBRUARY

At lunchtime I asked the girls how important they thought it was to have interests in common with a boy.

Lily put her head on one side. 'Well, it is quite cool if you both collect the same action figures.'

I tried to catch Megs's eye because we still haven't got to the bottom of what's going on with Arif, but Megs was busy opening her mouth. 'It's very important,' she said. 'You've got to have something to talk about; you can't just stare at each other's good-looking faces all day.'

I wasn't sure if she was making a point to Lily or to me.

'Like me and Cam. We've got things in common. We both love action films and R&B.'

'Getting back to me,' I said. 'I know that couples have to compromise about how they spend time together, but I'm not sure I want to go and watch Finn play football all the time. I'm not mad about sport, or the cold, or outside, and I don't want Finn to think that I'm one of those people who always does what the other person wants.'

'I don't think *anyone* thinks that you're that sort of person,' Megs smirked.

'Maybe it's about striking a balance?' Angharad suggested.

'Exactly,' said Megs. 'I sometimes go to football to support Cam and he supports me when I visit my grammy.'

This has put Cam in a new light for me. Megs's grammy has a gnome collection. Cam must really like Megs if he puts up with that. The gnomes have got names and everything.

'That's it then, isn't it?' Lily said.

'What is?' I asked.

'If you want to support Finn, but you don't want him to get the impression that you're going to follow him around like a puppy dog, then you could ask him to come to one of your things to support you.'

I thought about this. 'What exactly are my things? I'm not going to ask Finn to support me in torturing my little brother and I can't expect him to appear every time I could do with someone to back me up in an argument with Ramsbottom, can I?'

'What about the debating?' Ang asked.

So that's what I'm going to do. I will continue to support Finn with his football (unless, of course, it's raining) and he can support my debating club.

Just as long as Mrs Lloyd-Winterson doesn't die of old age before we can get it started.

SATURDAY 4TH FEBRUARY

Tonight I went round to Megs's house for a pizza with everyone. Megs's parents are so welcoming, unlike my miserable lot. Mum and Dad were having a cup of tea and an unnecessarily large slice of cheesecake when I came to tell them I was off. I pointed to Dad's plate and said to him, 'Is that a good idea considering your BMI?'

'A little of what you fancy is good for you, Faith.' And then he made a kissy face at my mother.

I gagged.

'Shouldn't you be making cutting remarks in someone else's house?' Mum asked.

I was going to bash her on the arm, but at the last minute I turned it into a friendly, if firm, pat. 'Since I'm not allowed a proper party, can I have seven people round for pizza next week?'

'No,' Dad said.

'Why not? Is it because you were shunned as a child so you can't bear me to be popular?'

'You won't be going anywhere for pizza if you take that tone, young lady,' Mum said.

'Anyway,' interrupted Dad, 'I'm sure we'd be delighted to have all your friends in the house . . .'

My heart leapt at this point.

'. . . It's *you* that we don't want hanging about making a mess!' Dad guffawed in a very unattractive fashion.

I silenced him with a look. 'Have you ever noticed how they always say that serial killers were quiet and kept to themselves? I expect their parents wouldn't let them have any friends round either.'

'If anyone ever describes you as quiet, it'll be me that drops dead,' Mum said.

Dad nodded. 'And if you do go on a killing spree don't be late back.'

'I'm just saying that you will definitely be blamed for everything I ever do wrong.'

And I swept out in quite a pointed fashion.

Then I stuck my head back round the door and said, 'Save me some of that cheesecake, will you?'

At Megs's house it was refreshing to be in the company of people who aren't idiots. Or at least the ones that are idiots let me tell them what to do.

When I arrived Cam and Ethan were already

there. Megs and Cam didn't have much to say because they were too busy snogging each other's faces off.

I smiled at Ethan, but he just said, 'Not out with Golden Boy?' and disappeared into the kitchen. Honestly, it seems like lately he's either snapping at me or staring into my soul. Can't he just have a conversation like a normal person?

Fortunately, Lily turned up soon after that. She was wearing a *Star Trek* T-shirt that she's had since she was ten.

'Whoa!' I said. 'That T-shirt's getting a bit … full, isn't it, Lils?'

Lily looked down at her spectacular bosom as if she'd forgotten it was there. She shrugged. 'Is Finn coming?' she asked.

'Nope. I am an independent woman who can do her own thing on a Saturday night.' I didn't mention that Finn hadn't shown any interest in what I was doing tonight. Apparently, his idea of us being official doesn't mean that we see each other any more often.

'I asked Arif,' Lily said.

I looked around as if I was expecting him.

'I was really hoping to see him tonight, but he had to go to his auntie's,' she explained.

'But it's got to that stage, has it?'

'What stage?'

'The seeing stage?'

'That's not really a very advanced stage though, is it?' Lily said. 'I mean, I'm seeing you right now.'

'You know what I meant. You're actually talking about meeting up. How come that hasn't happened before?'

'It never really seemed practical before.'

I coughed. Practical is not a word I expect to hear Lily say.

'I mean, I invited him to my last birthday party, but he couldn't come.'

I said, 'Right.' But really I was wondering what it could be that had changed in the last year that has altered Arif's feelings for Lily. And could the reasons possibly be located down the front of Lily's *Star Trek* T-shirt? After the pizza, I brought up some important business with Megs.

'Have you made any more plans for my birthday?' I asked. 'Because if you're going to find somewhere free and nice to throw me a party you'd better get a move on.'

She grimaced. 'So far the biggest package at the celebrations will be your self-importance.'

'I'm not asking for much. Just all my friends gathered round me and maybe a cheese and pineapple hedgehog or two.'

'Sorry, Faith, my mum said no, Lily's flat is too small and Ang is too timid to even ask.'

Westy popped up behind Megs. 'You can have your party at my house,' he said to me. Westy is very generous and always offering to give people stuff, although usually it's someone else's stuff.

'Won't your parents have something to say about that?' Megs asked.

'Nah, they'll be fine. They let me have people round all the time. They're just glad I've got mates.'

I didn't know Ethan was listening, but he called across the room, 'That's because you kept beating up the kids at nursery.'

Westy frowned at him. 'I was trying to *play*.' He gave me an appealing look. 'I didn't know my own strength.'

I patted his arm. 'I know, Westy.' I didn't want it to seem like it was all about me, so I waited several seconds before asking, 'Do you really think we could have my party at your house?'

He nodded hard. 'Yep. You lot can all come.'

'But surfer idiots are banned, right, Westy?' Ethan said.

Westy looked like a startled bunny. 'Erm ... I mean, Faith can ask who she likes.'

Ethan muttered something that I didn't hear, but I'm imagining that it was a rude remark about Finn. I didn't want to get into a fight about the guest list before we'd even settled the location.

'So your parents will really be fine?' I asked.

'Definitely.'

I do find Westy's mum delightfully welcoming and sane compared to my own bag-of-bats mother.

'He has got a big house,' Megs said.

Which is true. You would have thought that when the world was planning things out that it would have chosen a big house for me. I mean, I've got a very large personality. I'm emotionally stifled in our three-bedroomed semi.

Megs made Westy ring his mum to check. She said no more than thirty people and yes. Why can't my parents manage this kind of intelligent and quick response?

SUNDAY 5TH FEBRUARY

It was sunny today so I felt that this should be one of my football Sundays. Megs and I arrived a bit late. Finn only had a chance to say, 'Hi,' and then the whistle blew and he ran off with all the other boys.

'Wouldn't it be simpler if they were allowed to pick up the ball?' I asked Megs.

'That would be rugby.'

'Why don't they play that then?'

'Because they like football.'

I shrugged. People are very uptight about rules in sport. I prefer to mix things up a bit. They'd get better viewing figures for Wimbledon if they let the players break into a spot of pole-vaulting over the net occasionally.

'Last night was great, wasn't it?' Megs asked.

Which reminded me of what I'd been meaning to say. 'Yes. I assumed you were enjoying yourself snogging Cam because you made the same happy, slurpy noises that you make when you're having chocolate fudge cake, but now that you're at liberty to use your tongue for talking, instead of licking Cameron's eyebrows, we need to have a little chat.'

'I didn't lick his eyebrows! There may have been a small amount of eyelid kissing, but that's nice and romantic, so don't you dare make it sound all spitty and disgusting.'

'I have barely begun to tell you how it *sounded*. Anyway, just for once, this is not about your saliva. I want to talk about Lily. I'm worried about her.'

'We all worry about Lily.'

'I don't mean the normal stuff like will she remember to take the teaspoon out of her mug before she drinks her coffee and pokes her eye out? Or will we find her trying to rollerblade down the stairs again? I mean, I worry about boys.'

'What, that they'll have their heads scrambled with her chit-chat about badger bathrooms and that?'

'No, I mean she's had a bit of a growth spurt, hasn't she?'

When we started secondary school, Lily was

what Granny called a long thin streak of nothing: very tall and skinny and mostly knees and elbows. But recently she's, ahem, *filled out* a bit and has got that kind of curvy figure and long legs like ladies in black and white films. Also, she's finally stopped wearing her long blonde hair in plaits and now it sort of bounces round her face in a rather nice way. Obviously, I'm a flame-haired lovely (or vixen if you listen to Angharad, which, of course, I always do), and I suppose Megs is quite attractive if you don't have to listen to her talking too much, and Angharad ... well, Angharad is adorable, but Lily is definitely the gorgeous one.

'She is quite fit, isn't she?' Megs agreed.

'Yes, and I'm not sure about Arif. It seems to me that he's only got interested in meeting up with Lily since *certain developments* have occurred.'

'Certain developments? Do you mean boobs? Have you turned into Ang and picked up a fear of describing the female form?'

'All right, all right, the point is that I'm concerned Arif is more interested in Lily's boobs than the rest of her. Some boys are like that, you know, only interested in looks.'

'Oh yes, it's terrible, isn't it?' Megs said.

I nodded.

'Unbelievable the way some people only care about how someone looks.'

'Disgusting.'

'It would be pretty sick to date someone just because they had lovely sun-streaked hair, even if you had nothing in common.'

I hate it when Megs tries to be clever.

I said, with great dignity, 'I didn't start dating Finn just because of his hair.'

'No, the fact that he's gorgeous had something to do with it too!'

'So you do think he's gorgeous?' I said.

'He's got a nice face. That's not everything. I don't think you should choose your boyfriend just because of his face.'

'Oh, so Cameron's face had nothing to do with you wanting to go out with him?'

'Obviously, I fancy Cam, but I also find his personality attractive.'

'I find Finn's personality attractive.'

'What personality?'

'Don't be horrible.'

'I'm not trying to be horrible. I just don't want either of you to get hurt.'

I don't know how Megs managed to twist my friendly concern for Lily into her sticking her nose into my love life. I hardly spoke to her for the rest of the match. Why can't people just let me be happy?

MONDAY 6TH FEBRUARY

I got a text from Granny this evening. It said, **I'm outside**. It completely creeped me out. I could probably have her arrested for harassment.

Once I'd finished my magazine, I thought I'd better let her in. She made Dad fetch her a cup of tea and those chocolate digestives I've had my eye on, then settled herself on the sofa. 'Faith, here are those shorts I borrowed.'

I said, 'What do you mean those shorts you borrowed?'

She handed me a carrier bag and repeated, 'Here are those shorts I borrowed.'

I pulled out what were undeniably my black shorts, but I still couldn't stop myself from saying again, 'What do you mean those shorts you borrowed?'

'Your shorts. I borrowed them,' Granny said slowly, as if I was the mad one.

My brain was getting dangerously close to the idea of Granny-bottom in my clothes. In order to divert it I said, 'What do you mean those shorts you borrowed?'

'Your shor—'

'Hold it there,' Dad said. 'To save some time and repetition, Faith, I'm going to assume that what your granny means when she says those shorts that she borrowed is that she borrowed some shorts. Your shorts.'

It was like one of those scenes in a film when everything goes into slow motion and someone shouts, 'NOOOOOOOOOO!' and throws themselves in front of something precious.

Like a pair of River Island shorts.

Only it was too late to save the shorts. They had already been contaminated by geriatric bottom and now they were back. I clutched my shorts.

'I didn't have time to wash them,' Granny said.

I dropped my shorts.

'When you say borrow …' I asked in a very reasonable way, with only a hint of screech about my voice.

'Are we still here?' Dad said. 'I hate to hurry you, Faith, but in a few decades I'll have my own funeral to go to and I'd like to get some tea in before then.'

I ignored him. He thinks about nothing but his stomach and he can't even spare a thought for important issues like short-theft by an OAP. 'Because when you say "borrow",' I went on, 'it sort of implies permission from the person you are borrowing off. Otherwise, it's taking without consent. I could phone the police about that.'

'If she's really been wearing them, you could phone the police about indecent exposure,' Dad said in a very low voice.

'I didn't wear them outside!' Granny snapped. 'I just put them on for my Jump 'n' Jive class.'

Oh dear God. There was Granny-sweat involved now.

'And maybe for a while in the bar afterwards,' she said.

'You might as well have them,' I said, pointing at the poor scrumpled things. 'They're dead to me now.'

LATER

This must be what it's like when someone you love leaves.

I'll never look at another pair of shorts again.

LATER STILL

Although there was quite a nice pair with pockets in the New Look sale.

TUESDAY 7TH FEBRUARY

Today, in Music, Mr Millet split his trousers. It was brilliant. It's like the universe wanted to make up for the trauma I suffered yesterday.

WEDNESDAY 8TH FEBRUARY

At lunchtime a Year Seven with a ski-jump nose and sticky-up hair told me Miss Ramsbottom wanted me in her office. I said, 'I've told Miss

Ramsbottom before that I cannot sacrifice my education just because she's trying to cure the sickness in her soul by surrounding herself with youth and beauty at all times.' I leant towards the Year Seven, whose mouth had fallen open. 'My looks are a curse to me. Be thankful that you look like one of those little troll dolls.'

She backed away from me, swivelled on her tiny troll feet and fled.

I decided I might as well brighten Ramsbottom's day and headed off to her office.

'I hear you've been causing trouble in the PE department,' Miss R said, without so much as offering me a biscuit.

'What? That business about me suggesting we wear padded suits for gymnastics? If you'd ever had Megs's rear end coming at you as she did what she thinks passes as a cartwheel, you'd agree with me. It's an issue of health and safety, Miss Ramsbottom. I know you take that sort of thing very seriously because I can think of any number of exciting activities I've suggested that you've said no to, just because they involve a few explosives or a bungee jump.'

Miss Ramsbottom made a noise in her nose. 'Just leave these matters to the PE staff in future. They're a good deal more qualified than you are.'

I doubt that will still be true by the time I reach

the end of Year Eleven. I'm pretty sure that the PE department haven't got a Maths GCSE between them to bounce about with a ping-pong bat. I think the reason they disallow so many of my goals in netball is because they can't count past six. But I didn't say any of this to Miss R because, like all delusional, middle-aged women who think they can get away with a blunt-cut fringe, the truth pains her.

Miss R wasn't done with me. She sat down regally on her spinny chair like it was a vampire throne and said, 'I hear from Mrs Lloyd-Winterson that you're keen to set up a debating club.'

'Oh yeah, really keen. It's all sorted now. Nothing for you to worry about.'

'On the contrary, Faith, I find that keeping an eye on your exploits always turns out to be a time-saver in the end.'

I really don't need Miss R watching me. 'I'm sure Mrs Lloyd-Winterson knows what she's doing.'

'Nevertheless, before we go ahead with the club, I would like you to understand that I will be monitoring its progress. I look forward to watching you perform.'

I frowned. 'When you say "watching you", do you mean "you" as in the whole wonderful bunch of teen debaters or just wonderful me?'

'I will be watching *your* performance, Faith.

Whether you are wonderful or not will help me to assess how seriously you're taking this endeavour. It will also have a bearing on my comments on your end-of-term report.'

Which is hilarious because being good at arguing has never got me a good report before. I just smiled politely.

It must have been a good polite smile and not the one that Granny keeps telling me she expects to see on a 'wanted' poster one day, because at home time we saw that a sign-up sheet for debating club had been pinned on the activities noticeboard. The first meeting is after half-term. I'm glad that things are moving along, but I'm not sure that I approve of this free and easy membership approach; we could end up with any old Icky in the club.

I said to the girls as we walked home, 'There must be some way that we can keep Icky away from the sign-up sheet.'

'Or maybe we can keep the sheet away from Icky!' Lily said triumphantly.

I thought she might be on to something until she said, 'We just need some kind of spell . . .'

'What if we covered the sheet up?' Angharad asked.

'That's not bad,' I said. 'Perhaps we could find someone to stand in front of it every time Icky walked past.'

'I'm not sure anyone has got that much time on their hands, Faith,' Megs said.

'I don't know about that. I've never seen the cleaning lady do anything other than tut. She could do that at the same time as blocking the sheet, couldn't she?'

'That's not going to work, Faith.'

'Or Limp Lizzie – she's not exactly an asset to any of her lessons, is she? If she's going to quietly mope for the whole school day, there's no reason why she couldn't do it where I tell her to.'

No one replied so I went on.

'Or the Food Tech teacher. I'm sure she'd enjoy an actual purpose to her miserable existence for once or . . .'

At that point I realised that I was talking to myself. It seems that people can only cope with a small amount of my mind-blowing wisdom at a time. I should be gentler with my stupid friends.

LATER

We never did solve the problem of how to keep Icky away.

Maybe some sort of bug spray?

THURSDAY 9TH FEBRUARY

I went into school this morning in a very businessy mood. I can be businessy if I want to, especially if the business is nice stuff for me. At break time I said to the girls, 'We need to discuss my birthday.'

Megs sighed. 'We never talk about anything else at the moment.'

Angharad patted my arm. 'We're not going to forget your birthday, Faith. You wrote it in all our planners.'

'And you sent us a reminder last week,' Lily said.

More evidence of how efficient and businessy I am. I don't know why my mother ever calls me disorganised.

'The problem is that my birthday falls in half-term,' I said.

Lily grinned. 'That's good, you'll be able to have a lie-in and get your little brother to bring you breakfast in bed.'

There are many things that Lily gets completely wrong and one of them is little brothers. She's always thinking that Sam could be of use to me or that I've got some sort of non-aggressive feelings towards him.

'I'm not saying that I won't enjoy the extra snooze time,' I said. 'What worries me is that I won't be able to milk my birthday for all it's worth.'

'What do you mean milk it?' Angharad asked.

'Oh, you know how it goes: "Can I have one of your crisps? It's my birthday," or "Can I push in front of you in the lunch queue? It's my birthday," and "Please don't scald me with the molten lava of your hatred, Miss Ramsbottom. It's my birthday."'

They nodded. Everyone knows that you can ask for a few cheeky favours on your birthday. I mean, I ask for cheeky favours all the time, but I find that you're much more likely to actually get them on your special day. 'So you can see how unfair it is that my birthday is in half-term. I won't see anyone to extract my birthday offering from them.'

'You'll see us,' Lily said. 'We'll come round.'

'Yeah, but most people won't bother about my birthday unless I'm there to rub their faces in it.'

'Maybe your birthday won't be in half-term next year,' Ang said, as if that was the end of it.

'I'm going to be more proactive than that. I've decided that this year ...' I paused for effect. '... I'm going to have a pre-birthday day.'

I waited for a round of applause.

'That's nice,' Lily said, then she got out her Maths book. 'Ang, can you explain this algebra to me?'

'Wait a minute! Don't you want to hear about my plans?'

'Do we have to do anything?' Megs asked in what I felt was quite a whiny way.

'No. You can just encourage others in their generosity.'

Lily turned back to her Maths book.

'Although, obviously, you'll need to purchase a gift.'

'I've already got your birthday present,' Ang said.

'Yes, but you'll need a pre-birthday day present.'

'What, another one? I'm saving up to take a tourist trip into space,' Lily said.

'Won't that take forever?'

Lily shrugged. 'I'm young. There's plenty of time. But it would quicker if I didn't have to buy extra birthday presents.'

I pursed my lips. 'It doesn't have to be much, just a token.'

There was some more muttering. Honestly, they want to watch it or I'll dump them for some friends who are more giving. In both the spiritual and the birthday chocolates way.

FRIDAY 10TH FEBRUARY

Tonight's the club night. Although I'm not sure that anything they can do with lighting or smoke machines is going to make the hall look like a club, so they may as well call it a school disco.

For once, my jailers are allowing Megs, Ang and Lily to come round and get ready here. They did make up all sorts of ridiculous rules about not shrieking or bouncing on the bed so hard that plaster falls from the ceiling in the sitting room. Honestly. I mean, what's a gathering without a bit of bed bouncing?

My parents' fascism aside, I'm really looking forward to tonight. It is a completely official date for me and Finn.

SATURDAY 11TH FEBRUARY

So much happened last night.

The girls came round early and we all got ready. As we were coming downstairs, Dad called, 'Let's see your party frocks then! I've got the camera out.' He went a bit pale when he saw what we were wearing. I think he thought that we'd be in satin and frills. He looked at Mum.

'It's perfectly normal,' she said. 'Or at least as normal as teenagers get.'

Which is a bit of a cheek coming from a fully grown woman who owns a china unicorn.

Dad managed to keep his grieving over the maturing of his only daughter down to a low muttering and he drove us to school without doing anything else embarrassing.

It turns out that whoever was in charge of decorations knew exactly what you need to convert a school hall with wooden floorboards and floral curtains into a cool and sophisticated club environment: signs. There were signs about chewing gum, signs about not spilling drinks, signs about where the loos were. The overall effect was more like an optician's than a club. Not that I've ever been to a club, but I imagine black velvet sofas and fancy mirrors. We were stuck with gym benches and posters about basketball. But what's important is that everyone was there.

Everyone.

And they all got to see me on my date with Finn. There was even a bunch of St Mildred's girls.

'Who let them in?' Megs asked when she caught sight of Cherry.

'They let in anyone with a ticket,' Angharad said. 'The money's for charity.'

Megs sniffed. 'You'd think orphans would have higher standards.'

'Actually, it's for guide dogs,' Angharad said.

'That explains it,' Lily said. 'They can't see.'

I was going to attempt to explain guide dogs to Lily, but I was interrupted by Icky who yelled, 'Hey, Faith!' from the table where she was sitting. 'Just because it's for charity doesn't mean that you have to dress in clothes that came from the Cancer Research shop.'

I gave her a hard stare. 'I hope we raise enough money for a lot of guide dogs; we're going to need them if you keep blinding people with the glare off your pound-shop jewellery.'

Then my lovely friends formed a huddle round me and we completely ignored any further squeaking from Icky until Megs said, 'Oh my God, look!'

We all turned round.

'No, don't look!'

We all pretended to admire the ceiling.

'Just don't be obvious,' Megs hissed. 'You'll start her off again.'

'What is it that we're looking at, but not looking at, Megs?' I was expecting to see Mrs Webber tongue-duelling with Mr Millet by this point.

'Icky's feet.'

Icky had stood up and made her way round the table so that we could now clearly see that she was wearing the most ridiculous pair of high heels. I really do mean high. Six inches at least. They almost doubled her height. She must have had to climb a stepladder just to get into them.

'They look painful,' Ang said.

Lily nodded. 'They're not even nice.'

They weren't. There was a ring of spikes around the ankle. They looked like something a Viking would use in battle.

'Maybe she's trying to keep people away from her toes,' Angharad suggested.

I nodded. 'That's understandable. She doesn't want anyone to know that she's got trotters instead of feet.'

Just at that moment, Icky topped things off by deciding that she wanted a drink. She left her band of annoying girls and walked off to the refreshments hatch. I say walked, but actually she had to bend her knees and throw out her arms just to keep her balance. She tried to use speed to suggest confidence, but it was more of a trot than a strut. Essentially, she looked like a drunken pony on a tightrope. I laughed so hard that I hope I haven't spoiled my phone footage with all the shaking.

When Finn arrived, I got separated from the girls for a while, but I didn't mind because Finn was being super chatty and attentive. Also, he was looking really good. He was wearing a T-shirt that seemed to showcase his collarbone. Even that boy's skeleton is attractive. I wasn't the only one who'd noticed how gorgeous he was looking; every time I turned round, I could see dozens of girls' eyes fixed on him. Some of them didn't just look. Some of them wanted to chat. I suppose that it's to Finn's credit that he talked to everyone that wanted to speak to him rather than swatting them away like the blood-sucking insects that they are.

I was wondering if we could set up some sort of force field to keep back dribbling girls when I spotted Megs, Cam and Ethan working their way across the hall. I waved. 'Come and sit with us!'

Ethan looked at the people sitting at my table:

sporty boys and hair-flicking girls. 'Sorry, Faith, the light bouncing off this lot's fake smiles would give me a migraine. We're going to sit with Westy.' He pointed towards the back of the hall. 'If you get tired of listening to people tell you how great they are, you should come over.'

He turned away and Cameron followed him, pulling Megs by the hand. Megs mouthed sorry and said, 'I'll see you in a bit, yeah?', leaving me on my own. I mean not on my own obviously: I was sitting next to my lovely boyfriend. But I wished the gang had stuck around. I don't see why Ethan couldn't put aside his dislike of people who can run faster than him for once.

Finn asked me about my day and we had a nice chat about why parents are obsessed with the tidiness of rooms they're not even allowed to enter, but when he went off to get us some drinks I was left with his friends and the large crowd of girls they'd attracted, and I was a bit stuck for something to say.

'I like the fairy lights,' I said to Josh.

He nodded.

'It's a good night, isn't it?'

He nodded again.

Then a girl interrupted me to say to Josh, 'I saw you playing basketball the other day. You were amazing.'

Which was obviously the key to Josh's voice box because he started going on about jab steps and skip passes.

I could see that Finn had been waylaid on his way to getting our drinks so I decided to look for the girls. I got as far as the steps up to the stage when a voice in my ear said, 'Where's the bar?'

It was Ethan.

I pointed. 'It's less of a bar and more of a hatch.'

Ethan looked round and saw Mrs Webber trying to open a packet of straws behind the serving window that connects the hall to the kitchen.

'I was going to suggest whisky and soda,' Ethan said, lounging against the stage, 'but I think weak lemon squash is more likely.'

'I've often wondered about the lemon squash market,' I said.

'Yeah, it's entirely supported by schools and the Guiding movement.'

'Makes sense,' I said. 'Explains why teachers always look so sour.'

'That's their disappointment in the youth of today,' Ethan replied, 'but the squash doesn't help.'

We talked for a while. I was really pleased because I haven't had a proper chat with Ethan for ages, but, just when I was really starting to enjoy myself, he said, 'Better do the rounds. I'll never make it as a corrupt MP unless I get the support of the unwashed multitude.' And he sauntered off.

Which was fine because Finn was coming over to dance with me. I hardly even noticed that the unwashed multitude that Ethan was talking to most were a bunch St Minger's girls.

That's his business. I was having a great time with Finn. My boyfriend who I like loads.

Dancing with Finn really was great. He looks amazing when he moves. I got tingles every time we touched hands or bumped hips.

Megs and Lily came back from the loos and joined us to show off their dancing skills. Or at least Megs did. Lily mostly showed off the backs of her knees and the price sticker on the sole of her shoe while she repeatedly did scissor kicks.

'Where's Ang?' I asked Lily.

'Dunno. She said she was going to look for Elliot.'

After a bit, I said to Finn, 'I'm boiling. Do you want to go outside for a bit?'

He smiled. 'OK.'

I was steering us through the hordes, thinking that maybe outside there'd be a bit of snog action, when I finally spotted Angharad. She was sitting on a chair, all by herself, looking miserable.

Finn squeezed my hand. Part of me was already outside with my arms round him, snogging for

England, but I couldn't just leave Ang. I turned round to get Megs's attention, but she and Lily had already disappeared. Maybe Ang was all right; maybe she was just taking a breather? I looked over at her again. She hunched her shoulders and bit her lip.

'Listen, Finn, I've just got to see Angharad. It's important. Can we do this in a bit?'

'Sure, OK, Faith.'

Before he'd got three steps from me, I saw a Year Eleven swoop down and start smiling all over him.

Angharad didn't even look up when I sat down.

'You OK?' I asked.

She looked at me and then back at the dance floor. Between bobbing heads and waving hands there was Elliot. Dancing with a curly-haired girl.

'Oh. Well, they're just dancing, Ang. Maybe you could dance with him next?'

'How? I'm not like her. She just walked right up to him and asked him!'

'I thought after the New Year party you were feeling more confident with Elliot?'

'I was, but I'm never going to be like that, am I?'

She pointed at the curly girl who was flinging her arms out and grinding her hips.

'You shouldn't compare yourself to other people, Ang! I mean that girl does look confident and outgoing ...' I paused to watch her twitching her bottom about, 'and like she's got a small animal attacking her in the knicker region, but you're quieter and more dignified. Those are good qualities too.'

Angharad looked unconvinced.

'You're also really kind and considerate and thoughtful and generous and brainy and pretty and sweet. And there are lots of people, including boys, who think that makes you a great person to know.'

'I've just been feeling a bit ... left out. It's so busy and noisy here.'

Which I thought was one of the best things about it, but obviously Ang wasn't enjoying it.

I looked at the dance floor again. Finn was dancing with Josh and a couple of girls. I really wanted to be the one dancing with my boyfriend, but I squashed down my dancing desires and said, 'Do you want to go back to my house instead, Ang? We could watch a film and eat chocolate and do impressions of curly-haired girls who wave their arms about so much that they accidentally pick their dancing partner's nose.'

Angharad looked over. Elliot was jerking his face away from the girl's flailing nails. She laughed. 'That's OK, Faith. I'm staying the night with Lily. I don't mind waiting for her.'

'Why don't we go outside and get a bit of air then?'

'I'd like that.'

So we went outside and sat on the wall and I reminded Ang how amazing she is.

When we'd cooled down, we came back into the entrance hall where Icky's idiot friend was attempting to pull one of the Viking shoes off Icky's swollen trotter.

'It won't budge; you're just going to have to wear them for the rest of the night,' Icky's friend said.

When Icky saw us, she snatched her foot away and attempted to look casual. 'Have you lost your tiny boyfriend?' she asked Angharad. 'Did you put him down and forget where you left him? I hope someone doesn't step on—'

I shoved Icky backwards. How dare she talk to Ang like that? 'That's enough, Vicky! You're clearly just jealous of Angharad's poise and her ability to attract boys.'

'I can attract any boy I like.' She narrowed her ratty eyes. 'You know, Faith, you really shouldn't leave your boyfriend unattended.'

'Shut up, Vicky!' Ang said.

'Finn's not a laptop,' I said to Icky. 'He's not going to get stolen just because some nasty thieving types like to try and pick up anything that's not nailed down.'

Icky sneered. 'I don't think he needs to be stolen. He's been running after me for ages.'

She is so full of herself. 'Running *away* from you. Remember, there's a difference.'

She turned to her dopey friend. 'It's pretty clear Finn's looking for action.' She looked back at me. 'He's obviously fed up of kissing you.'

What the hell? My blood was starting to boil. 'I know you're obsessed with me and like to follow me around, Vicky, but I don't recall you actually being present any time Finn and I have had a private moment.'

'I don't need to be; he told me all about it. He said you stopped kissing just to show him a picture of a cat or something.'

It was all I could do not to flinch. How could she know that? Had Finn really told her?

'You can tell Finn likes Vicky from the way he looks at her,' the idiot friend said.

'Faith's the one he's going out with,' Ang said.

I knew I should say something, but I just couldn't believe that Finn had discussed our private snogging. To add to my humiliation I noticed that Ethan was lurking nearby. How much had he heard? He was looking at Icky.

'Be fair, Vicky,' Ethan said. 'Finn might be a dumb blond, but he does at least have the power of speech, unlike some of your boyfriends.' He walked towards her. 'In fact, now that I think about the way that last one used to lumber along grunting,

I'm pretty sure he was a zombie, which would explain why he was attracted to you, because you've got the stench of decomposing flesh about you, haven't you?'

Icky's mouth had dropped open.

'Faith's not worried about Finn; he can tell you to move your rotting carcass along just as well as I can.'

That shut her up.

One of the things I really like about Ethan is his ability to make Icky disappear. She stropped off with her friend.

I looked at the floor. I could feel myself getting very warm again. Had Finn really told Icky I'm a rubbish snogger? Am I a rubbish snogger?

Ethan didn't seem uncomfortable. He just said, 'What do you reckon? Vicky is actually deceased.'

'It would explain why you can see her bones through her skin,' Ang said.

Ethan nodded. 'And the state of her hair.'

'The lack of warmth, compassion and basic human decency,' I said.

Ang and Ethan laughed. I tried to join in.

'You all right?' Ethan asked.

I wasn't going to tell him that I was devastated that it seemed that Finn had been talking about me with Icky. 'Fine! Just taking a breather with Ang.'

Ang squeezed my hand.

'Hi, Angharad,' Ethan said. 'Actually, Elliot was looking for you just now.' He glanced at her tear-stained face. 'You know, he really likes you.'

It was nice to see Ang smiling again. 'Oh,' she said. 'Oh. I ... I might just go and find Lily.'

'Why don't you find Lily *and Elliot*,' I said.

Ang nodded and hopped off, looking a lot more cheery.

'Did Elliot tell you he likes Angharad?' I asked Ethan.

'He doesn't need to. I see in all directions. Like God.'

'Or a fly.'

'You don't need to be a maggot-laying, disease-spreading insect to see that Angharad and Elliot like each other. Although it would explain why Icky seems to know.'

I snorted. 'You know everything, don't you?'

He grinned.

I took a deep breath. 'Thanks for just now. You did an excellent job of putting Icky in her place.'

'Oh, stop,' he said. 'Any truly brilliant person could have done it.'

Even though Ethan was cheering me up a little bit, I couldn't stop thinking about whether what Icky said was true so I said, 'I think I'll get back to it.'

'OK. Listen, Faith.' He put a hand on my arm. 'Don't let Vicky get to you.'

'I won't.'

I walked back into the hall to look for Finn, but I was strangely aware of the patch on my arm where Ethan had touched me.

I marched straight up to Finn and asked him, 'Did you speak to Vicky?'

'Vicky? Yeah,' he said, as if engaging troll girls in chit-chat was a perfectly acceptable thing to do. 'She's nice, isn't she?'

Nice. He thinks Icky is nice. 'Did you speak to her about us kissing?'

'I don't think so.' He screwed up his face in concentration. 'Oh right. Vicky asked me what it's like going out with you. I said you're always making me laugh, like last week when you we were, you know, and you stopped to show me that cat wig. That was really funny.' He smiled.

I didn't smile. 'In future, do you think you could not talk about us snogging?'

He looked confused. 'But I like snogging you, Faith.' He took a step closer to me so that we were almost touching, but I wasn't going to forget Icky's sneering face that easily.

'I'm not sure that you give people the impression that you enjoy kissing me if you tell them I'm all weird and break off in the middle to talk nonsense.'

He took hold of one of my hands. 'I'm sorry I

upset you, Faith. I was just saying you're cool and funny.'

I could see that he didn't really understand what the issue was.

He pulled me closer to him. 'It doesn't matter what other people think, does it? Because you know I like you, don't you?'

Maybe it is stupid to care what Icky thinks. She just makes stuff up to annoy me anyway. And, after all, Finn had been saying how funny I was.

'Just please don't talk to other people about us kissing again, will you?'

He shrugged. 'OK. Is it all right if I do this?' He slid an arm round my shoulders.

I was still all tensed up, but I let out a breath and tried to relax. I know Finn didn't mean any harm. He's just too nice. He can't see that people like Icky always have an ulterior motive.

By the time the DJ put on the last song at the end of the night, I had pretty much completely forgiven Finn. Icky, on the other hand, I will never forgive. That girl is poison.

The whole gang got up for the last dance (although Ethan had disappeared by this point. I wondered if he'd gone off somewhere with one of the St Minger's, but then I realised that if he wants to make poor choices that's his business). Westy tried to insist that it was traditional for red-headed girls to dance the last dance with boys whose names begin with 'W', but I told him I was already booked. Ang and Elliot were shuffle-dancing within three metres of each other, so I take it that their relationship is going well.

We were all bopping away and I looked up and there was Miss Ramsbottom on the balcony. She was dressed all in black and looked as if she was about to unfurl her bat wings to swoop down and feed on the blood of the young. Had she been up there all night? I hope she didn't notice that impression I did of her.

Finn put his arms round me while we were dancing and I felt better than I had all evening. I just hope Icky stays right away from him.

SUNDAY 12TH FEBRUARY

I was supposed to be going shopping with Megs today, but her grammy has had a fall and is in hospital. I hope she's all right. Grammy does always make you admire her gnomes, but she is quite fun for an old person and always liberal with the biscuits.

Mum sent me upstairs to catch up on homework, but then Sam wandered into my room like a fly into a Venus flytrap, so I said, 'Do you want to play a game?' in a friendly and entirely non-threatening manner.

'Why?' he said, stepping backwards. 'What are you going to do to me?'

'Oh, Sam, you're so suspicious. Anyone would think that I'd harmed and ridiculed you before.'

'You have. A lot.'

'What does Mum always say?'

'Don't put that there? Who's eaten all of this? Am I talking to myself?'

I nodded; she does say all that in quite a shrill voice, quite often. 'She also says you've got to start each day afresh.'

Sam was unmoved.

'It's more of an endurance test really,' I said. 'But if you're not brave enough ...'

He took another step into my room. 'What do I have to do?'

'We have to see how long we can bear terrible trials.'

'Both of us?'

'Yep.'

'What's the first one?'

'Just a minute.' I dashed down to the kitchen and gathered a few supplies. When I came back, I said, 'Stick your tongue out.'

'What for?'

'First test. How long can you bear mustard on the tongue?'

Sam grinned. 'Easy.'

But there's a difference between a blob of mustard on your hot dog and a great fiery layer of it painted on your tongue. After a few seconds, Sam's eyes started watering and his nose began to run. To be fair, he held on quite a long time before rushing to the bathroom to rinse his mouth out.

'Well done, Sam!' I called after him. 'You might be weak in the head, but at least you've got a tongue of steel!'

When he came back, still dribbling and wiping his eyes, he said, 'Your turn.'

I looked at him in mock surprise. 'What's that?'

'Your turn. How long can you take the mustard?'

I smiled. 'Oh, I'm not doing it.'

'But you *said*. You said we'd both do it.'

'No, I said that we would both bear terrible trials.'

'And you haven't done yours!'

'Yes I have,' I said while I bundled him out of the door. 'I've had you in my bedroom for fifteen minutes. It was a terrible trial putting up with you for all that time, but I went the longest under unbearable conditions so I'm the winner.'

As I slammed the door, Sam's face was purple.

I don't think it had anything to do with the mustard.

LATER

I should thank Sam for helping me not to worry about Grammy. I'll show him my gratitude by not kicking, punching or poking him for twenty-four hours.

MONDAY 13TH FEBRUARY

Megs's grammy has got to stay in hospital for a few days, but she's OK, which means I was able to worry about something else this evening: tomorrow is Valentine's Day.

For several years, I've assumed that all I needed to make me perfectly happy on Valentine's Day was a boyfriend. But now I realise that it's not enough. What I really need is a boyfriend who will notice something like Valentine's Day and do something about it. I'm not sure that Finn even knows that such a thing exists.

I should probably just be grateful for the fun we have together.

LATER

But I see no reason why I can't have fun with my boyfriend *and* a card. And maybe a thoughtful gift or three.

I'm just saying.

TUESDAY 14TH FEBRUARY

Nothing in the post this morning. No one stopped

me on the way to school to give me flowers and no one sent a singing telegram into my Maths lesson. Cameron walked all the way over to our school gates to give Megs a single rose wrapped in cellophane and ribbon at lunchtime.

By the time I got to Geography this afternoon, I was starting to feel really depressed. I sat down at the table and Lily gave me a chocolate heart.

'What's this for?' I asked.

She grinned. 'Because I love you.'

Which just goes to show that you should not forget what really matters in life.

True friends.

And chocolate.

WEDNESDAY 15TH FEBRUARY

I met Finn in Juicy Lucy's after school. When we said hello, he gave me a kiss on the cheek. This made me feel quite sophisticated and I hoped everyone else had noticed how me and my boyfriend just throw the cheek kisses around like that. I told him all about Mr Hampton nearly setting fire to his own beard in Chemistry and Finn told me about someone driving off the top of a skyscraper in the film he watched last night. (I tried to find out what the car was doing on top of the building in the first place, but Finn was a bit hazy on the details. I think he sort of dips in and out of TV. He needs a loud explosion to get his attention.)

The thing I like about chatting with Finn is that I never feel like I've got to say anything really brilliant. We just sort of ramble along. Sometimes we run out of things to say, but he doesn't seem to mind that either. At one point I plucked up the courage to say, 'So Megs was going on about her Valentine's rose from Cameron yesterday.'

Finn looked blank.

'You know, it was Valentine's Day yesterday.'

'Oh. Right.'

'I was going to get you a card. I didn't know if you like that stuff.'

He shrugged. 'Cards are cool. I don't know about that Valentine's thing. It's like everybody has to do the same thing on the same day?'

I sort of understood what he was saying so I nearly just said 'Yeah', but I didn't really mean 'Yeah' and, you know me, I like to be clear so I said, 'I think it's a nice idea. It's good to tell people how you feel.'

He thought about this then he picked up his cookie and handed it to me. 'I feel like I think you're really nice, Faith.'

Which is actually way better than a rose wrapped in plastic.

THURSDAY 16TH FEBRUARY

Granny came over for tea. She poked about at the bowl of mixed leaves Mum put on the table and said, 'What's this?'

'It's rocket and baby spinach leaves with watercress,' I said.

'Don't be patronising,' Dad said.

I don't know why everyone mistakes my helpful voice for a patronising one. I can't help it if there are a lot of stupid people who need to be told things. Slowly.

And then Dad said, 'It's salad,' to Granny, which I thought was much more patronising.

'Salad used to mean some lettuce from the garden, a few pieces of cucumber and a tomato cut into quarters,' Granny said.

I nodded politely, which was a mistake because it gave Granny the idea that I wanted to hear more.

'The first time your grandfather took me to a restaurant on a date they cut the tomato into the shape of a flower and put a pinch of cress on top of my salad. We thought that was very fancy.'

I thought that if I heard any more about glamorous vegetables I might lose consciousness so I said, 'How's your boyfriend, Granny?'

She batted her eyelashes, tossed her hair around like a St Mildred's girl and said, 'Which one?'

Outrageous. I finally manage to get a boyfriend and Oldie Pants McAncient has to outdo me with her pack of wrinkly gentleman friends.

'They are all ...' She threw out a hand in a sweeping gesture as if she was talking about the population of a small country. '... Very well.' She sniffed. 'Except Malcolm. He's having a hip replacement.' She jammed a chicken leg into her mouth. 'Ows ors?' which I took to mean, 'How's yours?'

I gave her a stern look to let her know that I didn't approve of her showing off or talking with her mouth full. But I'm not sure she noticed because she'd got her false teeth stuck in the chicken and was trying to pull them loose.

'How is my boyfriend?' I repeated. 'He's very fit and healthy. No false bits. Just shiny hair and glowing skin, boundless energy and never wears his trousers pulled up under his armpits.'

Granny narrowed her eyes at me. 'There are some things that an older boyfriend does better.'

'Like what?'

'Pays with his credit card. Drives a car. Flies you to Switzerland.'

When I say something clever, I'm pretty sure that people find it enlightening. When Granny does it, it's just plain annoying.

'Yeah, well,' I said, 'I bet none of your

boyfriends can jump the library steps on their skateboard.'

Granny peered down her nose at me. 'Why would I want them to?'

I had to admit that she had me there so I passed her the garlic mayonnaise. Let's see what her boyfriends think of her breath after that.

FRIDAY 17TH FEBRUARY

Today was my pre-birthday day. When I'd assembled my minions at lunchtime, I said, 'What have you got for me?'

Lily handed me a tiny package. I unwrapped it, hoping for a diamond pendant, but inside was one of those plastic chips that you get in the amusement arcade when you win a game. When you've collected about a thousand, you can swap them for a prize.

Lily had given me just the one.

It was worth a thousandth of a giant teddy.

'Thanks,' I said. 'What am I supposed to do with it?'

Lily spread her hands. 'I don't know. I thought it was what you wanted.'

'Why would I want one of these? Why would anyone want one of these? I'm not sure anyone even wants a thousand of them because, once you've got over the excitement of a giant teddy, there isn't much you can do with it ... Except maybe leave it in your brother's bedroom doorway late at night so that it casts a terrifying grizzly bear shadow ...' Actually, I was warming to the idea of the giant teddy, but it still didn't excuse the token.

'When I said I'd already got you a present for your actual birthday day, you said that this pre-day thing present didn't have to be big. You said it was just a token.'

Sometimes I wonder why I bother to spend hours lecturing Lily in the art of being a normal person; it's clearly not making a dent in her insanity. 'I meant like a *token* box of chocolates or a *token* tenner. Not an *actual* token.'

Lily shrugged. 'Mr Hampton was right when he said that you need to work on your clarity.'

I gave her a punch in the arm.

Which I think made things pretty clear.

Ang said, 'I've got part of your present now and you can have the other bit on your other birthday.'

That seemed fair enough. When I opened the package, it was an earring. Just one. A tiny toadstool. It's pretty cute, but I fear that she's taken the surprise out of the second part of the present. Unless Lily's loopiness is catching and the second present isn't the matching earring. In which case there'll be more punching to do.

Megs gave me a box of Roses.

'That's more like it,' I said. 'See? This is why you get to be top friend.'

Megs shoved me. 'And there was me thinking it was my wit, charm and lively conversation.'

'Well, it's not your modesty, is it?'

Then I crammed an Orange Cream in her mouth to stop her from saying anything else.

I enjoyed my pre-birthday day a lot. I might have a post-birthday day later on in the year.

SATURDAY 18TH FEBRUARY

Finally, it's half-term. I swear the holidays are getting further and further apart. I went out for pizza with Finn to celebrate. I thought about inviting the gang along too, but apart from Cameron that lot seem to struggle to chat to Finn. I don't know why; I find that as long as you don't use too many long words Finn is prepared to talk about pretty much anything.

'I love the holidays,' Finn said. 'I really like that big long one.'

'Yeah, that's the best. Although sometimes my dad makes us go and see my cousins. They live in the middle of nowhere and it always manages to rain when we're there. Even in August. I wish we were going somewhere hot.'

'Mmm, the sun is awesome.'

'Where do you go on holiday?' I asked.

'My mum likes Portugal and my dad likes France. Me and my brother like anywhere with good surf. Some years we end up going to three different places, then everybody's happy.'

Which just goes to prove that I was right when I told Mum that the secret to a more harmonious family life is lots of money. She seemed to think it was something to do with love and compromise. I pointed out that if we were rich she'd be able to pay me to love Sam and compromise with her.

'I like to go surfing whenever.' He touched my hand and gave me a lovely smile. 'Hey, some of us are going to Cornwall in the summer. Maybe you could come for a bit. We stay in a hostel so it's not crazy expensive.'

I wasn't sure how much thought Finn had put into this suggestion, but it's always nice to be asked.

'Who's going?' I asked

'Me, my brother, Josh, couple of my brother's mates. It's going to be pretty cool. Surfing, swimming, maybe some mountain biking. You'd love it.'

I wasn't sure about that list of activities, but there's nothing wrong with the beach; I certainly do enjoy lying around eating ice creams and watching boys splashing about in the water.

'Sounds great,' I said.

LATER

Well, why shouldn't I make holiday plans? My parents are always telling me I need to take more responsibility and I am practically an adult. As far as I can see, there's no reason why I shouldn't go to Cornwall with my boyfriend.

LATER STILL

Well, maybe three reasons: 1) I've got no money; 2) Mum; 3) Dad.

SUNDAY 19TH FEBRUARY

I'm feeling very positive today. Obviously, there's plenty of time for me to make some money before the summer and how hard can it be to convince my parents I am extremely mature and responsible before then?

When Dad forced me to lay the table for lunch, I said, 'I need a job.'

Dad raised an eyebrow. 'Because you're already fulfilling all your obligations at home and school so well?'

'There's no need for sarcasm.'

'What is it then? You want to contribute to the functioning of our society?'

'Don't be ridiculous. I want some money, you turnip!'

'I don't think you're old enough to do most jobs.'

'How can I be too young to work? I've been slaving away at the coalface of learning for the last ten years.'

Dad handed me the place mats. 'Indeed. And I'd happily send you down a mine, but there are laws. They seem to think the children of today are too weedy for such work.'

'Weedy? Listen, you've got to be made of pretty stern stuff to cope with double Chemistry on a Friday afternoon.' I frisbeed the mats into place, demonstrating my considerable physical skill.

'I think they worry about you getting too tired and not having enough energy for your education.'

'And where are these concerned people when Killer Bill is forcing me round the athletics track?'

'You could do some more chores around the house.'

I clanked the cutlery down on the table. 'I want a proper job.'

'I'm not sure I can think of anyone who'd want a fourteen-year-old—'

'*Fifteen*. I'm going to be fifteen in about five minutes and I can't think of anyone who *wouldn't* want an energetic and enthusiastic teenager in their workplace.'

'Yes, but that's not really an accurate description of you, is it?'

'Dad, you are forgetting the first rule of

parenting. Remember that the child *you* know is completely different to the child that the world sees. I am generally known as a helpful and hardworking type.' I grabbed some glasses out of the cupboard. 'Except for at school and Granny's house obviously.'

'What were you thinking of?'

'How about a supermarket?'

'You can't work in a supermarket.'

'Yes I can! Watch.' I demonstrated how I am quite capable of swinging a scanning arm and looking hacked off at the same time.

Dad whisked the water jug out of the way before I sent it flying. 'While it's true that you do look remarkably like those girls in the orange uniforms, I'm pretty sure you have to be at least sixteen to work in a supermarket.'

'Who wants to work in a supermarket when they're sixteen?'

'I thought you did.'

'I want to work there *now*, not when I'm sixteen. I'll have been spotted by then.'

'Spotted? Spotted for what?'

'I'll leave that to the spotter. No one likes being told how to do their job. I know I won't. When I get one.' I sighed. 'So what can I do? I'm prepared to do anything, absolutely anything.'

Dad handed me a dish of vegetables to put on the table. 'How about a paper round?'

'I'm not doing that.'

'You said anything.'

'I meant anything that doesn't involve getting up at the crack of dawn.'

'Maybe you could go to work with Mum. She was saying that they need someone to sort out their stockroom.'

I rolled my eyes. 'I can't do that I'm afraid.'

'Why not?'

'You know what they say. Never work with animals or parents.'

'That's not what they say! It's animals or children.'

'Don't be silly.'

The conversation went on like that all through lunch. My idiot family were extremely unhelpful. Between them they only suggested seventeen different jobs and none of them were realistic. Mum got quite shirty in the end and said I was being too fussy. I said, 'I don't think I'm being unreasonable. There's nothing wrong with having aspirations.'

'It's a Saturday job. It is unreasonable to say that you won't do any washing, cleaning or tea making and that you can't work with old people.'

'Or pets or snivelling babies,' I reminded her.

Mum shook her head as if my phobia of bad smells counted for nothing.

'Well, if you could think of some sensible

suggestions, I'd appreciate it,' I said. 'Try focusing on the fashion world or the cutting edge of the pharmaceutical industry. That sort of thing.'

Mum and Dad exchanged a look that I'm choosing to believe was a shared expression of their pride in my high standards.

LATER

I've done a bit of research. There don't seem to be any suitable vacancies at Yves Saint Laurent or Pfizer. It's crazy that no one wants to employ a hard–working, responsible fifteen-year-old like me. It's selfishness, that's what it is. Old people want to have all the money and all the fun.

MONDAY 20TH FEBRUARY

This morning was our first day of half-term freedom and to celebrate I went with Megs to feed her grammy's cat.

'How is Grammy?' I asked.

'She's hoping to come home soon. She doesn't like the hospital food. I'm going to see her tomorrow.'

'It'll be good if she comes out this week because then you'll be able to visit a lot.'

'Yeah, if I find out when she's coming home tomorrow then I could put some flowers in her room.'

We gave the gnomes a polish, but there was nothing else to do. Grammy is a very tidy lady. I suggested we could clean out the biscuit tin, but Megs reminded me that Grammy is also a lady who counts snacks.

LATER

When Mum got home, she said, 'If you're serious about getting a job then I might have one for you.'

'Is it a diamond model or a crisp taster? Because I'm not really considering anything else at the moment.'

Mum did some of her extremely rude ignoring me. She behaves like a teenager sometimes.

'Oh, forget it,' she puffed. 'I'm not sure that you're a suitable babysitter anyway.'

'Babysitting?'

'Yes. You know Skye who works in the shop sometimes? She needs a babysitter. One afternoon a week, I think. But the way you're raising your eyebrows as we speak is making me think that you haven't really got the levels of patience required for this sort of thing.'

Honestly. It's not very nice when your own mother thinks you're lacking, is it? I decided to revise my no babies policy just to prove her wrong.

'Of course I can babysit,' I said. 'I've been a

baby, haven't I? Also, once, when I was doing a history project, I had one of those toddler-taming programmes on in the background. I learnt tons about what to do with children from that.'

'Like what?'

She had me there. The only thing I could remember about that programme was that they had such ugly curtains and sofas that I thought they should concentrate on sorting out their hideous decor before they worried about the children.•

'Come on, Faith, what do you do with small children?'

'Erm, give them some broth without any bread, then whip them all soundly and send them to bed?'

'Very funny.'

'Seriously, Mum, don't worry. Any old idiot can look after children. After all, they let you and Dad do it, don't they?'

LATER

Mum eventually agreed that I have definitely got the required skill set to provide care and entertainment for a toddler. Well, what she actually said was, 'There's no denying that you are still quite childish yourself.' Either way, I managed to convince her to ask Skye if I can have the job.

TUESDAY 21ST FEBRUARY

I rang Megs this afternoon, but she didn't have much to say. So I thought I'd cheer her up by talking about the good times ahead. I said, 'Now that it's February, it's practically the summer holidays. Maybe we could plan a trip to somewhere exotic. Of course, I might be going surfing with Finn. He usually goes to Cornwall.'

I could almost hear Megs's eyebrows go up. 'Cornwall?'

'I hear it's very nice in the summer.'

'You think you're going to go to Cornwall with Finn?'

I didn't much like her tone. 'Well, nothing's finalised.'

'Yeah, because your parents will definitely let you go off on holiday with your boyfriend.'

'His brother and his friends will be there.'

Megs laughed in quite an unkind way. 'I'm sure that the addition of some eighteen-year-old hotties will make the whole thing more acceptable to your mum and dad.'

'Good job I've got a while to talk them round then,' I said.

'For goodness' sake, Faith! Why do you have to live in the clouds all the time? There's no way you'll be going on holiday with Finn; do you even think you'll still be with him in the summer?'

'Of course, I mean—'

'You've already told me that he's boring.'

'I did not! I just said that sometimes he tells me the same thing twice, but—'

'And what about Ethan?'

I stiffened. 'What about Ethan?'

'See! You can't even be honest about that. You live in a fantasy world; you just pretend everything's brilliant, but it isn't and I'm sick of it.'

And she hung up on me.

I was furious. I rang her back ready to tell her exactly what I thought of her, but when she picked up the phone and said, 'What?' there was a little wobble in her voice.

I found myself saying, 'Is everything all right with Grammy?'

It turned out that Grammy had had a bad night last night. The doctor said they can't talk about her going home at the moment.

'She looks terrible,' Megs gulped. 'She's lost more weight. I hate to see her like this ... and ...' She let out a sob.

'It'll be all right, Megsie. Grammy is a very strong lady. When can you see her again?'

'I said I'd go back tomorrow.'

'Shall I go with you?'

Megs took a deep breath. 'Yes, please.'

LATER

I hope Grammy will be all right.

LATER STILL

I know it's a bit late to make resolutions, but I might make one to ask people how they are before I launch into everything that's happening with me.

EVEN LATER

And I might make another one to be a bit nicer to my granny.

WEDNESDAY 22ND FEBRUARY

Megs is feeling happier. Grammy had a better night and was feeling a bit perkier when we saw her today. She had enough energy to tell us that hospital staff ought to take an exam in how not to talk to old ladies like they're children, but she got tired quite quickly so we didn't stay long. The doctor told Megs's mum that he thinks Grammy is 'progressing'. That sounds positive.

When we were walking home, Megs said, 'I'm sorry if I was mean to you yesterday.'

'You don't have to apologise. I know that you were worried. I'm sorry that I was banging on when you were thinking about more important things. I should have asked you about Grammy.'

'I should have told you. I just didn't know what to say.'

'You know that you don't even really need to use words, don't you?'

She nodded. There may have been some cuddling.

I took her back to my house for a snack.

'What is that?' she asked when I presented her with a tiny scene featuring a mini gingerbread man standing next to his Bourbon and chocolate finger cottage.

'It's biscuit art.' I screwed up my nose. 'Do you really think that I'm living in a fantasy world?'

'Well, obviously,' she said, biting into a Bourbon door, 'but that's part of your nutty charm.'

'You can always bash me over the head if you need me back on earth, all right?'

She tapped me on the forehead with a chocolate finger. 'Thanks.'

THURSDAY 23RD FEBRUARY

I went to meet Skye and her rug rat today. I was pleased to find that her ramshackle house is massive. This means that if the brattling is noisy I can just pop it five rooms away. I was surprised to find a hippy like Skye living in a big house; I thought that they mostly went for yurts and solar-panelled caravans and that, but Skye told me that she inherited the house from her uncle. Also, it's mostly falling apart; there are bits of plaster missing from some of the walls and damp stains on the kitchen ceiling. Skye herself could do with a bit of sprucing up. She reminded me of my mum – tassel-skirted and hair all over the place.

'I just wanted to get to know you better, Faith,' Skye said, grasping my arm.

My elbow is an area that I usually reserve for Finn and for jabbing people with, but I didn't want to seem unfriendly so I just smiled.

'Faith,' she said, drawing it out. 'Such a solid name. Earthy.'

This sounded a bit like she was calling me muddy, which I think was hypocritical coming from someone who later told me that clothes don't need washing nearly as much as people think they do and that it's kinder to the planet not to use washing powder.

I had to be careful in the hallway. There were bits of crystal dangling from the ceiling, twirling about and nearly blinding me every time they caught the light. Fortunately, Skye soon waved me into the sitting room, which seemed to be constructed entirely of books, and I don't mean the good kind about vampires or dystopian societies where teachers are kept in cages. I mean the kind that my mum sells in her shop. They all had words like 'spiritualisation', 'empowerment' or 'cosmic' in the title.

Mini-Skye was much as I expected. He looked like he was made of unbleached organic cotton. And grime.

'What's your name?' I asked in the voice I normally use on Lily when she's had too much Fanta.

Mini-Skye spat at me.

Skye clapped her hands. 'He's really getting the hang of interaction, isn't he? His name is Tolde.'

'Toad?'

'Tolde. Tol-*duh*. It's the name he whispered to me when he first started communicating with me from the womb.'

I didn't have anything polite to say about her whispering womb so I tried a smile at Tolde the Toad and he held out the book he was chewing to me.

'Oh, that's all right,' I said, 'I've just had lunch.'

'Have you had much experience with children?' Skye asked.

'Oh yes, I'm always looking after my little brother. You know, reading him stories, making him snacks.' Which wasn't even untrue. Just last night I threw a packet of peanuts at Sam and read out the bit on his report where his teacher said he can't sit still. 'He also enjoys playing with my Pretty Ponies.'

Skye told me that she was going to be teaching a Women's Poetry class at the community centre on Tuesdays and that she needed someone to look after Tolde between four and seven. Then she showed me round the house and explained what Tolde likes to do.

'He doesn't have a routine or a strict bedtime. I don't believe that children should develop to a schedule. I think they should be free to explore and grow and play, don't you?'

'Oh yes.' I only wish that Mum would take a few pointers from Skye. Imagine what my life would be like with no bedtime, and parents who wanted me to be free to play.

When we came to the end of the tour, I was wondering how to bring up money. I'd done such a good job of sounding like I enjoyed playing with children just for the fun of it that I didn't want Skye to discover that I'm actually a cash-hungry desperado.

Fortunately, she eventually got to it herself first, I had to endure some rambling about Tolde's soya milk and emergency numbers, but when she finally mentioned a figure I was quite pleased. Skye really does stand by her hippy philosophy that she'll give anything for her child. I wonder if that will be true of Mum the next time I ask for a tenner?

Back at home Dad asked how the job interview went.

I said, 'Well, they're not perfect, but I'm prepared to give them a go.'

'I was under the impression that you were the one being interviewed.'

Which was a different angle on things I suppose.

LATER

If that was a job interview then I don't know why grown-ups make such a fuss about them. I could have talked about myself all day.

FRIDAY 24TH FEBRUARY

It's my birthday! I love birthdays.

This evening, after we'd had tea, Sam switched off the lights and Mum and Dad brought out my birthday cake. I blew out the candles and picked up a knife. 'I expect you three won't want much after that big meal.' I sliced three slivers and handed them round.

'Hey!' Sam said. 'How come you get a big bit?'

''S my birthday,' I said through a mouthful of cream. 'And I need my strength to vanquish you in the Birthday Fun.'

In our house birthday cake is always followed by Birthday Fun, which consists of a series of highly skilled and fiercely fought trials to establish which family members are superior and should be rewarded with the ultimate prize.

Malteasers.

'Oh, I thought you'd be too old for that this year,' Mum said.

My heart sank – a birthday isn't a birthday without Birthday Fun – but then Dad said, 'I don't think Faith will ever grow out of being overly competitive for chocolate rewards.' And he produced three boxes of Malteasers from the back of the cupboard.

'I'll have Mum on my team,' I said.

Mum beamed. 'It's nice to be wanted.' And she gave me a hug.

'Don't get cocky,' I whispered in her ear. 'You're just better at cheating than Dad.'

Sam ripped open a box of Malteasers because, as well as being the prize, the Malteasers are actually integral to all the games.

'Let's start with blow football,' Sam said.

I fetched the straws and a couple of Tupperware tubs for goals. I may have chosen a larger one for me and Mum.

It was a pretty good game. There was some discussion about whether I should be sent off for inserting a straw into Sam's ear canal, but I maintained that it was fair punishment for him sitting in our goal. As usual, Dad objected to my goalkeeping technique, but we all know that goalkeepers are allowed to touch the ball with any part of their body, so obviously it's completely acceptable for me to prevent a goal by eating the ball. The final score was 4–2 to me and Mum.

Next we played Malteaser Mountain. You get a minute to build the tallest Malteaser structure you can. It's quite hard to get rolly-round Malteasers to stay put, but I have perfected a highly scientific method: I lick them. If you get the chocolate just a little bit melty then they stick together pretty well. When the egg timer went off, I had managed a very impressive mound of Malteasers. Dad had made a line and Mum was still chasing hers across the floor. Dad whipped out his ruler.

'Let's start with Sam,' he said.

I turned round to check my little brother's effort. He'd basically jammed a pile of Malteasers into the corner of one of the armchairs. Because of all the support, it was actually quite a tall pile.

'That's cheating!' I said.

Sam scowled. 'No one ever said we couldn't use the sofa.'

'It's not technically against the rules,' Dad said, measuring the mound.

'Mine's higher anyway,' I said.

Dad held his ruler next to my marvellous structure and nodded. 'Yes, Faith's i—'

My poor pyramid lurched. And then tumbled down. I must have been a bit overenthusiastic with my licking; one of my Malteasers had carried on dissolving right down to a honeycomb pip, making the whole thing unstable.

'Sorry, Faith, looks like the points go to our team for that one,' Dad said. He didn't look very sorry.

Before I could have a proper whine, we moved on to How Many Malteasers Can You Fit in Your Mouth? When I got to eleven, I could see Mum positioning herself ready to do the Heimlich manoeuvre, but eventually, as usual, Dad and his colossal gob won. I came second, Mum third and Sam in last place where he belongs.

'Right,' I said, 'the scores are even. It's all down to the Flour Cake Final.'

Dad filled up a mixing bowl with flour and then turned it out on to a tray so that we had a lovely flour 'cake'. I carefully placed a Malteaser on top. Then we had to take it in turns to cut 'slices' of flour away without knocking the Malteaser off. Soon all that was left was the Malteaser perched on a slim column of flour. It was my turn.

I gripped the knife with a firm hand.

'Watch it!' Sam said. 'Don't wave the knife about! If you get me in the eye, we win by default.'

'Maybe, but if you lose an eye I reckon I'll win every Birthday Fun ever afterwards because your depth perception isn't going to be up to much, is it?'

'Come on, Faith,' Dad said.

So I took the tinniest sliver off the side of the column of flour.

The Malteaser didn't even wobble.

'Good one!' Mum said.

'She didn't cut any flour!' Sam moaned. 'She did an air-slice!'

'Pigging heck, Sam, it's a good job I didn't take your eye out; you obviously can't see very well even with two unpunctured eyeballs.'

'Actually, Faith,' Dad said, 'I didn't see any contact between the knife and the flour either.'

I growled. 'Fine! I'll do it again.'

Unfortunately, because I was giving Sam a stern look instead of watching what I was doing this time, my hand shook, I cut too much and the Malteaser fell down into the piles of collapsed flour cake.

'Yes!' Sam punched the air.

I punched Sam.

Then, because I am a really good sport who doesn't get hysterical and squeaky about losing, no matter what the St Minger's netball team might say about me, I took my punishment and leant into the flour to pick up the Malteaser with my teeth.

'I'll get you next time,' I said to Dad, blowing flour out of my nostrils. 'And your little helper monkey too.' I pointed at Sam who was doing a victory lap round the room.

'You played very well,' Mum said to me, handing Dad and Sam their winners' boxes of Malteasers. 'We were robbed in Malteaser Mountain.'

Dad had the grace to look a little shame-faced about that. I reckon he knocked my pyramid with his stupid ruler.

'Actually, Faith, you can have these,' he said, passing me the box, 'for your forward-thinking Malteaser architecture.'

'Thanks, Dad.' I looked at Sam.

'What? You're not having mine,' he said.

I smiled angelically. 'That's all right, little bruv. It's all about the fun really, isn't it? Come here.'

And I planted a hand on either side of his head and gave him a big kiss on the nose.

'Ahh,' said Mum, 'that's sweet.'

Yes, I definitely am a loving older sister. And the fact that I rubbed a large quantity of flour into Sam's hair while I was showing him affection was (probably) entirely accidental.

SATURDAY 25TH FEBRUARY

Granny came round to give me my birthday present. It was a watch.

I said, 'Thank you very much. If I ever lose my phone and Megs at the same time, and actually care about being punctual, it will be very useful.'

Granny said, 'You're welcome.'

I've got a strong suspicion that she doesn't listen to a word I say.

Fortunately, Granny didn't stay long because she had a date. I said, 'I've got a date too. With my young and attractive boyfriend and my friends who are throwing me a party for my birthday.'

Then I drew her a picture with labels just in case she hadn't been listening to that either.

Once Granny had gone, I started my party prep. Now I'm all ready to see my adoring friends. I will write about how fantastic it was tomorrow.

SUNDAY 26TH FEBRUARY

I absolutely love parties that are especially for me. I decided to turn up a little bit late so that everyone would get to see me arrive. When I stepped into the kitchen, no one noticed me for a moment, but then Westy came barrelling through the mob of people shouting, 'FAITH!' which was quite effective in getting everyone in the room to turn round.

They all started whooping and cheering. It was

mad. And very enjoyable. You can see why people will embarrass themselves on reality TV to try and get famous. There's something quite nice about being in a room full of people who are all pleased to see you.

Especially certain people. Seeing Finn's face light up as he bounded across the room to kiss me hello was fantastic. Once everyone had finished patting me on the back and congratulating me for managing to be a year older, Megs put on our favourite song and the whole room did some crazy jump-up-and-downy dancing.

Later on I sat down with Finn and he gave me my birthday present. I think maybe I shouldn't have got my hopes up for jewellery. We haven't been dating very long and it was a quite nice purse, even if the Hawaiian surf print wasn't necessarily what I would have chosen. Finn seemed really pleased with himself. He said, 'Because you love shopping! You can, you know, put your money in it and then when you buy stuff you can ... take your money out!'

I said, 'It's lovely. Thank you.' Because if I've learnt anything from my parents it's that the truth is sometimes best avoided if you want to make a relationship work.

After a while, the talking dried up a bit. You would have thought that given the array of outfits, snogging and dancing going on in front of us that he'd have had plenty to chat about, but every time I started a well observed remark such as, 'I hope she doesn't split those tight trousers,' or, 'He looks like my granny taught him how to dance,' Finn would just say, 'She's all right,' or, 'He's a nice dude.' I realise that this is because Finn is a nicer person than I am, but it does cut down on conversation a bit.

I was actually quite relieved when Megs skipped over and said, 'He's here! Arif is here! Come and see!'

I let Megs drag me away. 'Where is he?' I asked.

'He texted Lily to say he was almost here and she went out the front to meet him.'

I spotted Angharad and waved her over. We positioned ourselves by the door.

'What do you think he'll be like?' Angharad asked.

'He'd better be nice,' I said, 'and he'd better appreciate her. Most of the boys in here would love to be with Lily.'

Megs nodded. 'So what do you think is so great about Arif that he's the one that she chose?'

'I think she just likes him,' Angharad said. 'She talks about him a lot. And they've got their hobbies in common.'

I think obsessive sci-fi-series-watching is more

of a life choice than a hobby, but, judging by Arif's emails, it's true that they do like going on about the same geeky stuff.

'Maybe there's something we don't know about him,' I said.

'Maybe he's a teenage secret agent,' Angharad suggested.

'I think he'll be a juggler,' Megs said.

I fixed my eyes on the door. 'I was imagining him in a hat. And possibly some kind of crazy glasses.'

When Arif and Lily came in, Arif was not wearing, or doing, anything crazy, but his eyes were glued to Lily.

'This is Arif,' Lily said proudly to us all.

'Hi,' Arif said. 'It's nice to meet you. Lily has told me what great friends you are.'

Then Lily dragged him away to the drinks table.

'He seems nice,' Angharad said.

I wasn't going to let good manners and very shiny teeth charm me. I was determined to make sure he was good enough for Lily. 'Just keep your eye on him,' I said.

Becky and Zoe popped up then to give me their present (three lip balms in the shape of cupcakes) so I watched Arif from a distance. He didn't say much, but he smiled a lot. Later I was sitting with Finn and some of his friends. Finn was holding my hand, which was nice, but everyone was talking about Josh's new bike, which was less nice. I spotted Arif sitting by himself so I squeezed Finn's hand and said, 'Back in a sec.'

Arif looked up as I approached. He seemed nervous.

'Hi, Faith, are you having a good birthday?'

I nodded. 'So, Arif ... what first attracted you to my drop-dead gorgeous friend?'

He twitched like a startled rabbit. 'Er, I really liked her attitude.'

'I see. What about her attitude?'

'She's just so ... cheerful. Lily is the happiest person I know.'

There's no denying that Lily is relentlessly perky.

'Then I found out that she can list all the Doctor Whos and their companions in chronological order.'

He was trying to blind me with geek-speak. 'And that's a good thing, is it?'

'Everything about Lily is good.'

'If you thought she was so great then why didn't you visit before?'

'I wanted to come to her birthday party last year, but ...'

I folded my arms. 'What? Had something better to do?'

'I was a bit scared of meeting you all.'

'There's nothing to be scared of.'

He gazed up at me, standing there glaring down at him. But I wasn't going to be friendly until I was sure about him.

He bit his lip. 'I wanted to see Lily by herself, but it took me a long time to pluck up the courage.'

Lily herself appeared from behind me and said, 'Tell Faith about your stop-motion version of *Star Trek* using Lego.'

To be fair, when Arif tells a story involving sci-fi and Lego figures, he's a lot less rambly than Lily. But my in-depth assessment of his suitability as a boyfriend for Lily had to wait a bit while I did some dancing and cupcake eating and chatting and snogging with all of my lovely guests. (Apart from the snogging bit: I just did that with Finn.)

I was filling up my fifth plate at the snack table when I bumped into Becky.

'Good party,' she said. 'Some very nice boys.'

I looked round the room. The nearest group of boys were all trying to get the attention of one black-haired girl. One of the crowd of admirers was Ethan.

'Hey, isn't she that St Minger's girl that was at the club night?' I asked.

Becky nodded. 'She's called Dawn.'

'*Dawn?* Midnight would be more like it. She looks like the angel of death.'

'She is spookily pretty.'

Which wasn't what I meant. 'Why is she at my party?'

'She came with Ryan. She's his cousin.'

Which explains why I'm pretty sure I saw her at the New Year party too. I made a mental note to tell whoever organises my next party that it should be by invitation only. At least she hadn't brought Cherry with her.

'She seems to be enjoying herself, doesn't she?' Becky said with raised eyebrows.

I think I'd enjoy myself if I had eight boys hanging on my every word. Obviously, I don't need a pack of boys staring at me. I've got a lovely boyfriend. All the same, I was strangely relieved to see Ethan break away from the group to grab Westy by the neck and shout something in his ear.

Megs came scurrying over. 'I've been talking to Arif.'

'Oh, I think he seems lovely,' Becky gushed.

'He really is nice,' Megs said. 'I thought he'd be more Lilyish, but he's actually quite sane. What do you think of him?' she asked me.

'I haven't made up my mind about him yet. It still seems a bit convenient to me that he gets up the nerve to ask Lily out just when she blossoms into womanhood.'

'Oh no,' Megs said. 'You've got that wrong. Totally wrong.'

'How do you know?'

'Hold on a minute.' And she wove her way between people to where Arif was talking to Cameron. When she came back, she held out a photo to me. 'Look at this,' she said.

'What is it?'

'It's a picture of Lily that Arif carries around in his wallet.'

I took a look. It was at least two years old. Lily was looking extremely long and skinny in a very dodgy pair of dungarees. She was also wearing a baseball cap and sticking out her tongue. It wasn't the most flattering picture I've ever seen of her. 'Why has he got this?'

'Lily sent it to him. It's the only photo he's got of her.'

'He's probably seen other pictures of her ...' Thinking about it, I realised Lily isn't one of those people that posts pictures of herself looking gorgeous. In fact, in most of the photos I've seen of Lily online she's wearing a terrible hat or doing something stupid with fruit.

Megs gave me a pointed look. 'He might have seen other photos, but this is the one that he takes with him everywhere.'

'Oh.'

'He says every time he looks at her in that picture it makes him happy.'

'Oh.'

'He also said that Lily's the smartest girl he's ever met.'

My mouth dropped open. 'That's it then,' I said. 'He really does like her.'

'Yep.'

When I said goodbye to Lily and Arif, I leant over to Arif and said, 'You have my permission to be Lily's boyfriend, but make sure you look after her, OK?'

He still looked a bit scared of me. 'You don't just mean when she's crossing the road, do you?'

'Well, that might be a good idea too, but don't make her sad or I will hunt you down and squash you.'

Arif swallowed. 'Honestly, you won't need to hunt me down. I promise I won't ever do anything to upset Lily.'

And then he gazed at her with such adoration that I suddenly felt empty inside. I looked around for Finn. He and Josh were balancing on the back of the sofa and pretending to surf. Finn waved. I waved back.

Waving isn't very soulful, but he did bring me another piece of cake and get Westy to put on my favourite song again. My boyfriend is very sweet.

LATER

There's something else that happened at the party. Something with Ethan. I wasn't going to write about it because I'm trying quite hard to forget it, but I have to try and sort out what happened in my head.

He didn't speak to me for most of the night, which is the first stupid thing he did. I happened to notice that he spoke to a lot of other girls. Which annoyed me. Not because I was jealous or anything, but because it was my birthday party after all.

After Megs had shown me Arif's photo of Lily, I went out to the hall to put some of my presents with my coat and Ethan was coming down the stairs.

'Hi,' I said.

'Hey, Faith, nice party that you've managed to get someone else to organise.'

'Thanks, I'll take that as a compliment.' But I wasn't sure that it was.

There was an awkward pause.

And then I said something stupid. Maybe I was fishing for a compliment, which was dumb because Ethan is not a big one for compliments. Anyway, the words just slipped out of my mouth. I said, 'Do you like my dress?'

'No,' he said.

Which is a very unkind thing to say to someone on their birthday. I expected him to follow it up with something else rude because Ethan can be pretty cutting sometimes; instead, he looked at me from under his curls and said, 'But I like you,' in this really low voice.

My anger died and my heart started thumping.

And then he took a step towards me and I really thought he was going to kiss me. I felt like I was in a film and the music was doing that swelling to a crescendo thing. I looked into his dark eyes and even though I was frozen to the spot everything inside me was leaning towards him.

But he just twisted his mouth into a sort of sulky half-smile and said, 'Happy Birthday, Faith.'

What on earth? What the hell was that about? I think he did it on purpose just to wind me up. I can only hope that my face didn't look like I was hoping he'd kiss me.

Even though, I think, I kind of was.

I didn't see him again after that. I did enjoy my party, I really did, but why did Ethan have to mess with me?

MONDAY 27TH FEBRUARY

Going back to school today has been a nasty shock after all the fun and birthday cake of half-term. Sensible people treat the second half of the term as a gentle slide down to the next holidays. Not Miss Ramsbottom, but then Miss R is not like other sane human beings. She seems to think that our depressing return to school is a time for renewed energy and for starting stuff that I am quite frankly too tired to even be sarcastic about. First, she came round all the tutor groups informing us of the new rules she's thought up. I managed to block out most of them, but I did hear her mention something about wearing our uniform with pride and not accessorising it.

I said, 'Not even with a smile?'

She looked daggers at me. 'Of course you may smile. And if you're all in the correct uniform then I'm sure that the teachers will be smiling too.' She attempted to pull her death mask into a grin. I could almost hear her skin ripping. As smiles go, it was pretty thin.

But the one that Mrs Webber was doing behind her back was fairly broad.

Today's assembly was all about the Student Council. I didn't know that we had a Student Council. Judging by their startled bunny looks, as they shuffled about up on stage, they had only recently found out themselves. They seemed a bit stunned. I suspect that Ramsbottom has hypnotised them so that she can use them like puppets. Which is a new and subtle approach for the vampire woman in her manipulation of people. Usually, she just shouts, 'Do what I say!'

Anyway, the Student Council said that they're very interested in what we think about the way the school is run and what we'd like to see done.

Then they told us what actually is going to be done.

There didn't seem to be a consultation period between the two things.

So now that we have these brilliant minds championing the students' needs and fighting our corner to ensure that the school does its best for every member, what innovative and exciting changes do you think they are bringing about?

We're getting a suggestion box.

That is democracy for you.

LATER

Tomorrow will be my first time looking after Tolde the Toad. I sidled up to Mum and said, 'So ... this childcare business. Just give them a biscuit and build a pen of toys to contain them, is it?'

Mum gave me what she thinks is a piercing look. 'There's a bit more to it than that. Think of some games. Try to engage him. Talk about his toys. Ask him questions. Read him a story.'

It suddenly became clear to me why Mary Poppins was always bursting into song. She was obviously insane after spending so much time talking about stuffed animals and being forced to listen to children's answers to questions.

Mum shook her head. 'Just play with him and keep positive, all right?'

Sounds simple enough.

TUESDAY 28TH FEBRUARY

After school, Megs walked with me to Skye's house. On the way, I told her about what happened with Ethan at my birthday party, although, when I told her that I'd thought Ethan was going to kiss me, I tried to sound like I was horrified. Her eyes did a lot of bulging.

'Why do you think he did that?' I asked.

'Dunno, maybe he wanted to snog you.'

'But there *wasn't* any kissing. He never said anything about kissing. It was just that he was right in my face. I think he was trying to make me look like an idiot.'

'He doesn't have to get you puckered up for that.'

'Shut up! I reckon he was just trying to embarrass me.'

'Either that or he wanted to snog you.'

I was strangely pleased that Megs thought Ethan's weirdness means he likes me, although I still think he was just messing with me.

We'd reached Skye's house by this point. I rang the bell and Megs was about to disappear off, but I said, 'No, wait, you can see her crystal collection when she opens the door and, if we're lucky, she might let you stay.'

Skye opened the door wearing a rainbow tie-dye jumpsuit. Needless to say, Megs was not looking at the crystal collection.

'Hello, Faith, is this your friend? Come in, come in!'

Megs backed away. 'I was just ...'

'No, you must stay! Tolde will be delighted to have two playmates! And there's plenty of goulash in the kitchen for everyone.'

Ha! What could Megs say? We were both swept inside.

Tolde the Toad was sitting in the cupboard under the stairs building a tower of shoes.

'Isn't he creative?' Skye gushed. 'I don't like him to have those noisy plastic toys, because children play better with real-world objects, don't you think?'

'Mmm,' I said, as I blocked Toad from jabbing me in the leg with the heel of a sandal.

Skye kissed Tolde's knotty hair and picked up her raffia basket-bag. 'I'll be back around seven. Have fun! Eat goulash! Play, dance, create! Whatever makes Tolde's heart sing!'

Off she went, slamming the door, which made the whole ancient house sway.

Apparently, what made Toad's heart sing was for him to continue to jab me in the thigh with various shoes.

When he got bored of the shoes, he threw them down the hallway and started screaming and hammering the floor with his fists.

I looked down at him. His usually pink face was turning bright red. 'Do something, Megs!'

Megs looked around for something to distract him with.

She found a pot of bubbles in the sitting room beside a half-eaten banana on the mantelpiece. 'Look, Tolde!' Megs said in a soppy voice. 'Bubbles!'

Fortunately, Toad quite liked the bubbles and ran about smashing them with his favourite shoe.

'Ahh, look,' Megs cooed. 'He loves it when you blow bubbles. He's so cute.'

I didn't think he looked cute, but he definitely looked less like a tomato that's about to explode so I was pretty happy that we'd finally found something he likes. Toddlers are quite demanding. Personally, I only need a skinny cappuccino with cinnamon not chocolate, a selection of magazines and a large plate of doughnuts with most of the sugar brushed off to be happy.

The bubbles kept him busy for a bit. Then

feeble Megs ran out of puff and Toad shouted, 'Ooh ash! Ooh ash!'

'What's he saying?' I asked Megs. 'I don't speak baby.'

'I think he wants some goulash.'

So we sat him in his tall chair and gave him some goulash. Toad hadn't actually specified what it was that he wanted the goulash for. I assumed it was eating, but, as Skye keeps saying, Toad is a creative child, so instead of eating it, he painted with it. Megs and I watched with appalled fascination while he covered the high chair, his clothes, his face and his arms. Then he got a bit Jackson Pollock and started flinging handfuls on the kitchen floor.

Megs snapped out of her frozen horror and took the bowl away from him. 'No!' she said.

I remembered something Skye was banging on about last time I was there. 'His mum said she doesn't want to set up barriers to his exploring the world by using negative words like no.'

'More fool her,' said Megs, sounding a lot like her own mum.

Toad scrambled down from his chair and started stamping about in the splats of goulash. 'We'd better clean this up,' I said.

Megs's phone rang. She pulled it out of her pocket.

'It's Cam,' she said. 'Do you mind? Will you be all right?'

'It's fine. Tolde can help.'

'Really?'

'Yes, of course. Children need to learn about domestic duties early. My parents should have got me scrubbing the floor when I was tiny, but they were too lazy. It's all their own fault that I can't be bothered to help around the house now.'

Megs was already walking out of the room and saying hello to Cameron in a gooey fashion.

I ran the hot tap and started poking about for a cloth; when I turned round, Toady had pulled a packet of muesli out of the cupboard and was flinging handfuls up in the air like confetti. I remembered what my mum said about keeping it positive.

'There's a good boy,' I said. 'You're a good boy, aren't you? Put the muesli back—'

He tipped the packet upside down.

By the time I'd found the dustpan and brush, he'd managed to grab his beaker of milk off the table and pour it on the floor. I snatched up a tea towel and tried to stop the rush of milk towards the rug.

'Never mind,' I said through gritted teeth because I was remembering to be positive. 'We'll just sing a song, shall we? Five little ducks went swimming one day . . .'

I gave Toad a saucepan to play with and started on the blobs of goulash. Toad opened a cupboard and reached for the crockery. I abandoned the mucky floor and snatched one of Skye's hand-thrown pots out of his grubby fist. While I was putting it back, he dropped on all fours and started crawling through the remains of the milk puddle. What I needed was some of those calming bubbles.

'Megs!' I called. 'If you've finished your lovey-dovey chat, I could do with some magic bubbles in here.'

'Come on then, Toady,' I said, scooping him up. 'Let's keep cheerful ... *Ah!*' Tolde had grabbed a handful of hair on either side of my face and was attempting to pull my head apart like a Christmas cracker.

'*Megs!* Can you bring the bubbles?'

I picked up a wooden spoon and danced it about like a puppet. 'Hello, Tolde! I'm Mr Spoon. Why don't you let go of that hair and—'

Toad snatched the spoon and whacked me in the mouth with it.

'Megan! I need you to distract Tolde with the bubbles while I clean up.'

The sink was overflowing; I took a step towards it and skidded on a lump of goulash. Toad almost went flying out of my arms. I may have sworn a tiny bit at that point, which Toad must have disapproved of because he started howling.

'*La-la-la!* Ducky ducks!' I sang. 'MEGS! GET IN HERE NOW AND BLOW ME SOME PIGGING BUBBLES!'

And that's when I realised that Finn was standing in the doorway.

LATER

If I found someone attempting to clean up a very goulashy kitchen and child, I like to think that I would do something helpful like scrub one of them down or, at the very least, go and buy some emergency chocolate. I would not start banging on about how it's 'not cool' to swear in front of kids.

LATER STILL

I wasn't so cross with his comment that I didn't notice that Finn was looking super fine in a new blue top, but I've got to admit that I can think of people I'd rather see in an emergency.

WEDNESDAY 29TH FEBRUARY

At breakfast I said, 'Today is a leap day, which means a free day to do whatever you like with.'

Mum looked at me blankly.

'You don't normally get a twenty-ninth of February, do you?' I pointed out. 'So we should all count it as a gift of extra time to do something to gladden our hearts and make our spirits soar.' I stood up. 'So I'll be returning to bed with this ...' I picked up the Coco Pops packet, 'and this ...' I reached out for the tiny kitchen TV.

'Oh no you don't,' Mum snapped. 'Leap day or not, it's business as usual. You're going to school.'

I shook my head sadly. 'For a woman who claims to be at one with the world, I'm not sure that you listen very carefully to what Mother Nature wants for her children. Surely you agree that I ought to be out frolicking in the wild, not cooped up in a prison-like classroom? I need to feel the wind on my face and the earth between my toes.'

Mum took the Coco Pops out of my hand. 'You can walk to school in bare feet if you like.'

I think it's about time I threatened to call a social worker again.

MARCH

THURSDAY 1ST MARCH

We had the first meeting of the debating club today. Lots of people came. The news about boys being in attendance had obviously spread like wildfire. In a way it's nice to think that my ideas are so successful, but on the other hand I wish that the Year Elevens would find their own methods of getting near boys. Thank goodness we're safe from the St Minger's here. But unfortunately not from Icky, who was there early, strutting about the room. It's sad that she feels that she's got to keep thrusting herself in people's faces to remind them that she exists.

As if anyone could forget that monstrosity.

I was pleased to see that Ethan, Cam, Elliot and Westy had all turned up. Then I spotted Finn and my little heart leapt. Even though I spent quite a lot of time explaining debating, he hadn't seemed that keen when I invited him, so I was touched that he had turned up. Obviously, he does want to support me in my activities, which is nice. I also noticed a lot of envious looks from the Year Elevens when he greeted me enthusiastically, which was even nicer. I was less thrilled when I got distracted talking to Megs and Finn wandered off to say hello to almost everyone in the room. He seems to know a lot of girls. 'Does he have to be so friendly?' I said to Megs.

'I thought you told me that was one of the

things you like about him. Would you rather he was surly and stand-offish?'

I only gave her a small wallop because I was watching Ethan talk to Becky. I hadn't seen him since he managed to both insult me and nearly kiss me at my party. He nodded hello to me when the boys came in, but he didn't say anything. He seemed to have plenty to say to Becky. I didn't think they even knew each other that well.

Mrs Lloyd-Winterson went to the front of the classroom and waited for silence. She was pretty good at it. I wish I could achieve the same sort of quiet just by looking at Toady. She thanked us all for coming and told us what a super time we were all going to have, and then she explained about the debating.

'Every week we'll have two motions.'

'What's a motion?' Cam called out.

'Shh,' Westy said in a really loud voice. 'It's what you do in the bathroom.'

'What? Have a bath?'

'No, you idiot, have a poo.'

'The motion,' said Mrs Lloyd-Winterson in her best icy tone, 'is the issue we will be discussing. For example, I might say "Teenage boys are ill-mannered" then one team would propose the motion, that is, agree with it, and the other team would oppose it, that is, disagree with it. Each team is made up of two people.' She cast her beady eye round the room. 'Looking at how marvellously popular this endeavour is, I think that each person will have the opportunity to debate once a term. That means you'll really be able to throw yourselves into it.'

'What do we do on all the weeks our team isn't arguing, I mean debating?' someone asked.

'Then you will be the audience. Which is a vital part of the whole process; your votes will decide the winners.'

'Shall we get into pairs, Mrs Lloyd-Winterson?' I asked. I took a firm grip on Megs's wrist just to be sure of her.

'Well, yes—'

Before she'd even got the words out, people were grabbing at their besties.

'Oh no,' said Mrs Lloyd-Winterson. 'Oh no, that won't do.'

'What won't?' Westy asked, while tucking Elliot under his arm for safe keeping.

Mrs Lloyd-Winterson put her hands on her hips. 'I don't think we'll have you pairing up with your friends.'

My heart plummeted. She wasn't one of those evil teachers that thinks you do your best work when you're forced to partner up with your enemy, was she?

'Look like you don't know me!' I hissed to Lily. She started whistling and looking skyward. The well-known international sign for not knowing someone.

'No,' said Mrs Lloyd-Winterson again. 'I think the teams should have one boy and one girl; after all, that's what we've all come for, isn't it? A spot of fraternisation.' And then she *winked* at the doddering old fool that the boys' school had brought with them. I would have vomited, but I was trying to catch Finn's eye and, even though I had a good try the last time I got off a rollercoaster, I still haven't perfected throwing up and looking attractive at the same time. Finn was also whistling and looking skyward and I don't think he was even trying to pretend he didn't know anyone.

'Yes, everyone get into boy-girl pairs,' said the old man teacher.

I elbowed a few girls aside and tapped Finn on the arm. 'Shall we be a team?'

He grinned at me. 'Yep, sure.'

There were a lot of envious faces as I pulled up a chair next to him.

The rest of the room weren't getting on too well. Megs had grabbed Cam, Ethan asked Becky, which really annoyed me for some reason, and Icky threw herself at some poor unsuspecting boy, but other than that there was a lot of foot-shuffling, which was really very silly. It's the bold worm-girl that catches the boy-bird. Or something like that.

'Come on, come on!' barked Mrs Lloyd-Winterson 'Pair up!'

Nobody paired. So Mrs L-W started ploughing through the room, shoving random couples together. That started a bit of movement. A circle of eager boys formed round Lily, but she asked a boy with a robot drawn in biro on his arm and he nodded. Angharad and Elliot shuffled together and looked over each other's shoulders. I'm pretty sure that neither of them actually spoke, but maybe really quiet people have some kind of language that the rest of us can't hear.

Once we'd sorted out the pairs, Mrs Lloyd-Winterson made us watch a video of some boys in fancy blazers having a debate about whether kids should be able to divorce their parents. It was quite funny in places.

In the middle of it Finn leant over to me and I thought he was going to whisper something romantic, but he just said, 'We don't have to wear those jackets, do we?'

After that, Mrs L-W asked us for suggestions for motions.

I said, 'What about "School should be optional"?'

'Students should be able to sack rubbish teachers,' a girl at the back called out.

'No animal testing,' Ang said.

Pretty soon everyone was calling out suggestions. The boys' teacher wrote them all down on slips of paper. Then Mrs L-W talked to us about how to research our topic and how we shouldn't believe everything we read on the internet. She gave us a helpful sheet on getting started. I really don't need any help writing down my opinion in convincing terms, but I'm sure it'll be useful to stupid people like Icky.

Just before it was time to go, each pair had to pull a slip out of the rubbish bin. Finn let me choose. We got 'Nurses should be paid more than footballers'; we are opposing the motion, which means we have to disagree with it. I watched carefully to see who we'd be arguing against. When Icky stuck her hand in the bin, the back of my neck prickled. I don't believe in second sight and all that business, but the back of my neck clearly knows what it's talking about because it's Icky and her new friend that we'll be arguing against. Which is good because I find that I am at my best when I'm arguing with someone I detest.

Mrs Lloyd-Winterson said, 'I'll draw up a schedule, which will be displayed in both schools. Make sure you find out when your debate is and *prepare* for it.'

I can't wait to win our debate. I am fully

prepared. I've already had years of practice at telling people they're wrong.

FRIDAY 2ND MARCH

The debating timetable is up. Poor Zoe is first. Finn and I are second on the list, which means that we've got less than two weeks to prepare something that will impress Miss Ramsbottom.

I was checking out the rest of the list when Icky squawked in my ear, 'I don't know why you bothered to join debating club.'

I turned round to face Her Royal Scrawniness. 'You're right,' I said, 'it is a bit unfair on other people when I'm so obviously going to win.'

She snorted in an unattractive, snot-gurgling sort of way. 'How are you ever going to win a debate? By blinding people with your bright orange hair? Or are you going to knock them out with your skunk scent?'

'The only way you're going to get anyone to listen to you is by dressing up as a kitten. That won't be difficult since you're the right size and you've already got the claws.'

She sneered. 'I won't need to dress up. I'm going to beat you.'

'That's right, think positive, Vicky! Maybe you'll manage to convince yourself you're not an idiot.'

'Listen, Faith, when they're all applauding me,

you can kiss my feet. Because I'm way better than you.'

I've always said that Icky is delusional. 'Want to bet?'

'Yes,' she snapped. 'And if you lose you really can kiss my feet.'

'Actually, when *you* lose, you can kiss mine. Although that doesn't sound very hygienic. Make sure you wash your mouth out first. I don't want my poor toes getting contaminated.'

'It's a bet then.'

And she stuck out her twiggy little hand and I actually shook it.

I was right. She has got claws.

LATER

I rang Finn to make plans to vanquish Icky in the debate. At first, he seemed to have forgotten about the whole thing, but then I managed to jog his memory; I said, 'Remember we watched the video of those posh kids debating?'

'Yeah! The dudes in the jackets. So when do we have to get dressed up?'

'We don't actually have to wear anything special. We just have to write really good arguments and then present them to the group.'

In the end we arranged to meet in Juicy Lucy's tomorrow to discuss strategy.

SATURDAY 3RD MARCH

Finn isn't exactly what you'd call a strategist. He says we've got plenty of time to worry about the debate later. I am usually quite a fan of taking it easy on the homework front, but firstly, I really want to beat Icky, and secondly, I want to show Miss Ramsbottom how good I am so she can write me a good report and then my parents will let me have parties every week. So I'd quite like to get our brilliant speeches organised now. Unfortunately, I didn't really feel able to hit Finn over the head until he agreed with me.

He's not Megs after all.

I tried to listen to him chatting, but I just kept thinking about how awful it will be if Icky wins our bet. I said, 'Maybe when you've had a think about it you could email me your ideas?'

He shrugged.

'Because if we want to thrash Icky we should make sure we've got some brilliant arguments.'

And he said, 'Why do you want to beat Vicky?'

He said that.

He really did.

I didn't feel like explaining that a) Icky is a poisonous pixie who should be proved wrong at every opportunity, and b) I really like winning. So we finished our milkshakes mostly in silence.

There was no big goodbye snog, but Finn didn't even seem to notice that it was missing because he said, 'See you at football tomorrow?' in a perfectly cheerful voice.

How could anyone be cheerful when they've missed out on snogging me?

SUNDAY 4TH MARCH

I didn't go to watch Finn play football today. I'm still a bit cross with him. I don't know if it's fair of me to be annoyed that he didn't want to get on with the speech. Maybe not. It was his Saturday after all. I just feel that we've got totally different attitudes towards this debating thing. And towards other stuff. Like Icky.

And also sports, animals, siblings, music, healthy food and when it's acceptable to punch someone.

I called Megs, but she's visiting Grammy in hospital, so I'm going round to Lily's and I hope that she and Angharad will cheer me up.

LATER

I'm feeling a bit less miserable. Once we'd done the preliminaries (raided Lily's chocolate stash, opened cans of Coke, teased Ang about Elliot), I said, 'Lily, do you remember last term when you said that you didn't think that Finn and I were suited?'

'Yep. You're not.' Lily never worries about hurting anyone's feelings.

'You are a bit different,' Ang said, trying to soften the blow. 'But that doesn't mean that you two can't get on. Look at me and Lily.' And she threw her tiny arm round Lily's tall frame.

I don't know why I didn't think of it before: Ang and Lily are totally different.

'And what about your parents?' Ang asked. 'Your mum is ...'

'Crazy?' I offered. 'Surprisingly dim for someone with a child genius like me?'

'I was going to say a hippy. Your dad's not a hippy, is he?'

I snorted. 'No. He pretended to be when he first met my mum. His cousin made him go to Glastonbury Festival because he was the only one with a car and that's where he met my mum and she was all flowery and that, and she said she was a vegetarian, so my dad pretended to be one too. The next day my mum appeared from behind his tent when he was in the middle of eating a hot dog so he lobbed it into the bushes. His friend Nobby still calls him wiener-wanger Bill.'

Angharad laughed.

'What's a wiener?' Lily asked.

'A sausage,' Angharad said.

'Right.' Lily was quiet for a moment. 'What's a wanger?'

'A thrower,' I explained. 'You know, like wellie-wanging.'

'What's wellie-wanging?'

Now it's fair enough that someone might not have heard of wellie-wanging, but I went to primary school with Lily, so I know that she attended our school fête for seven years and I know that every year Mr Chowdhury ran a wellie-wanging competition. I have even watched Lily wang a wellie. Not that she wanged it very far. In fact, she kept slapping it against the ground, but still ... she has no excuse for her ignorance of wanging.

'You know,' I said. 'It's that competition that Mr Chowdhury used to hold to see who can throw a wellie the furthest.'

You could almost see the wheels turning in Lily's head. 'Oh! I thought that was wellie-*banging*.' She paused. 'That's probably why I never won a prize.'

I'm not sure that Lily's poor hearing is the real reason why she's never won any prizes.

'Anyway,' said Angharad, who is used to Lily's mad interruptions and quite experienced at getting things back on track, 'the point is that people don't have to be really similar to get on.'

I found this quite reassuring. Finn and I don't

need to be exactly the same. We complement each other with our opposite skill sets. I can help him with the debate and he can ... explain sport to me if I'm ever having trouble sleeping.

So I have spent this evening writing a truly brilliant speech that will knock Miss Ramsbottom's socks off and wipe the floor with Icky. I've emailed it to Finn so he knows which lines of argument I'm taking.

I may have also included a few suggestions for him. I hope that's not too bossy.

But being bossy is definitely one of my skills.

MONDAY 5TH MARCH
I have made a suggestion to the Student Council suggestion box. It said, 'I suggest that we get rid of the suggestion box.'

I told Finn about it when he rang me. He just said, 'Uh-huh.' He's not the most brilliant conversationalist in the world. But he did say later that he's looking forward to seeing me on Thursday. Angharad is right; Finn might not have my killer instinct, but he does have other good qualities like being sweet and nice and liking me.

TUESDAY 6TH MARCH
I don't know why anyone spends time with children unless they're being paid for it. When I look after

Tolde, I have to imagine five-pound notes in his hair to keep me going. It's really quite hard caring for a toddler. They've got such babyish ideas about what's a good way to pass the time. They won't even consider the more sophisticated pursuits that teenagers enjoy, like lying on the sofa and criticising the hairstyles of people in magazines. I don't think Tolde has ever lain down in his life. I suspect that he sleeps standing up, like a tiny skittish horse.

Anyway, because I am an incredibly patient person, I have finally found a few activities that both Toad and I enjoy, namely finger-painting and biscuit-eating competitions. I am educating him in the Impressionist school of Art (i.e. don't worry if it doesn't look exactly like the thing it's supposed to be) and he is teaching me how to put a whole Bourbon in my mouth without gagging.

It's all about the giving and the sharing.

And the biscuits.

LATER

And the making money so I can go on holiday with my gorgeous boyfriend. I wonder if any of the shops have got bikinis in stock yet.

WEDNESDAY 7TH MARCH

At lunchtime today, while Lily and I were waiting for Megs and Angharad, I asked if Lily had plans for her birthday at the end of the month. She said, 'I don't want a big party. I like it when I get to talk to everyone and I know Ang prefers smaller get-togethers, so I thought we could all go bowling. You know, us lot and the boys. And Arif's coming.' She beamed, and I thought it was because she was really happy about Arif, but then she looked down at her mushy shepherd's pie and her plastic cup of jelly with a blob of squirty cream on top and said, 'Yummy.'

'Yeah, moving on from your lack of taste buds and strange affection for rubbery food, I was going to ask you if you wanted me to organise you a pre-birthday day like me?'

She shook her head. 'I don't need extra presents. I feel like I've already been given loads of precious gifts.'

'Like what?'

'Arif, my health   this jelly.' She scooped up a spoonful. 'And my friends.'

Typical Lily. Not caring about presents is exactly the kind of misjudgement I expect from someone who ranks me below a wobbling dessert. She is bonkers.

'Besides,' said Lily, still beaming at her pudding, 'I wouldn't want people thinking I'm a pain in the bum like you.'

See? Totally mad. Talks utter rubbish.

THURSDAY 8TH MARCH

Today was the first official debate at debating club. I was a bit late because Mr Hampton was feeling lonely again and felt the need to keep me behind for ten minutes' company under the pretence that he wanted to talk to me about safety in the lab again. As if he hasn't already told me a hundred times that it's not a good idea to use a lit Bunsen burner as a sword.

When I arrived, Finn was talking to Icky. At least Finn was talking; Icky was attempting to stand as close as possible to him without actually climbing into his trousers. Although she might have tried the trousers thing if I hadn't elbowed her out of the way.

Mrs Lloyd-Winterson gave the debating pairs a bit of time to get sorted and told the rest of us to work on our own debates with our partners. Finn turned to me and said, 'Hey, it's really cool that you did our thing. You're going to be great.'

Which sounded rather like he thought that he didn't have to do anything.

I noticed Icky was jabbing a finger at her partner. She obviously wasn't afraid to take charge. I tried to take a more upbeat approach with Finn. 'So did my speech give you some ideas for yours? Are you nearly finished?'

He fidgeted in his seat. 'Er, your speech looked

really good and everything, Faith, but it was quite long and I didn't exactly get to the end of it.'

He hadn't read my speech.

'So ... I thought that since you'd probably covered everything I wouldn't need to write anything more.'

Seriously.

I took a deep breath. 'You *do* have to write something because it's a team debate and you're half of this team.' I like to think that I didn't sound too whiny, but to be honest there was a whine in my heart.

Finn just shrugged. 'OK. Yeah, I guess I could do that.'

I'm not sure that Finn is really into this debating.

I looked round the classroom. Ethan was reading from his notes and Becky was convulsed with laughter. I bet Ethan's speech is brilliant. I didn't get to say anything else to Finn because Mrs Lloyd-Winterson was calling the debaters up to the front. I felt a bit sorry for them. It's tough going first. Zoe was partnered by a quiet boy called Matthew, and they were against a Year Eleven girl called Olivia and a boy called Addy. They were debating whether teenagers should have the vote. Olivia got the giggles and Matthew kept tripping over his words, but Addy and Zoe were both really good. In the end Zoe and Matthew won, but it was really close.

I said to Zoe afterwards, 'You and Addy were both so good that I almost didn't know who to vote for.'

Zoe gave me a shove. 'Do you mean you nearly didn't vote for me? I'll remember that when it's your turn to get up in front of everyone next week.'

I patted her on the back in a friendly way. 'Obviously, I very quickly realised that you were, of course, far superior and why don't you have this Mars bar I found just lying about in Megs's lunchbox?'

At the end Icky smarmed off and called, 'Bye, Finn,' in a ridiculously syrupy way.

And Finn said, 'See you, Vicky.'

I don't understand why he likes her. I wanted to talk to Megs about it, but I knew that she'd say it shows that Finn and I are not suited. The thing is, I am not a quitter. I don't give up on people just because they're not perfect. Otherwise, I would have divorced my parents by now. Very occasionally, it has been suggested to me that there are cracks in my own brilliance. Therefore I am resolved to concentrate on Finn's positive qualities rather than the annoying bits.

FRIDAY 9TH MARCH

Mum has got some crazy idea that we should have

a family picnic this weekend. I said, 'Since we've just had Christmas and my birthday, I'm not really looking for a way to get into your good books at the moment, so I think I'll give it a miss.'

Mum drooped. 'I would just like our family to create some happy memories.'

I relaxed. 'Well, why didn't you say so?'

Mum's face lit up.

'I'm all for creating happy memories. We don't have to have the whole family in the same room to do that.'

'I would like us to spend time *together*,' Mum said in a growl.

'And I would like a trust fund and naturally frizz-free hair; you've got to manage your expectations, Mum.'

She narrowed her eyes. 'If I have to make it compulsory, I will.'

'Great idea There's nothing like bringing people together against their will. People hardly ever murder their relatives, do they?'

She gave me a sinister smile. 'Don't put ideas in my head.'

SATURDAY 10TH MARCH

I went to McDonald's with Finn. I thought that maybe we could have a look at his speech, but he didn't bring it with him. Not a lot of debate planning actually happened. There was some French fries eating and a lot of snogging. Normally, those are two of my favourite pastimes, but I couldn't help thinking about how we've hardly got any time left before our debate.

It's almost as if Finn has no interest in crushing Icky, ahem, I mean the other team.

I suggested that we have a run-through after I've finished babysitting on Tuesday.

LATER

I rang Megs. 'How's Grammy?' I asked.

'She's doing really well, thanks. They're talking about her going home next week. She told me to go round her house and dust behind the radiators.'

'She definitely sounds better.'

'Yep, it's great. How was your date with Finn?'

'Good. Fine. Really excellent.'

'So he's finished his speech?'

I was reluctant to tell Megs about Finn's lack of effort. He's a sweet, gorgeous boy who I wanted to date loads, so I'm not going to start moaning about him just because he isn't as keen on thrashing Icky as I am. So I said, 'Yeah, pretty much finished.'

'Is it any good? Becky says Ethan's is brilliant.'

I wrinkled my nose. 'Listen, Megs, you're always telling me to be realistic, so I am. It's true that Finn is not the world's greatest speech writer.

But he is my boyfriend and he is really nice. That's what counts.'

'I suppose so.'

She didn't sound entirely convinced.

SUNDAY 11TH MARCH

This morning Finn came to my house. Just turned up. No phone call. No text. No five-minute warning siren so that I'd have time to arrange myself attractively on the sofa or bludgeon my family to death and hide them in the shed where they couldn't embarrass me. Finn just rocks up and sits down to have a cup of tea and a chat with my mum. That's what I came downstairs to this morning. There he was, wearing a white T-shirt, looking like an angel, and there she was, all ratty-haired and withered. It was like Christmas mixed with Halloween.

'Hey, Faith,' Finn said.

'Um, hi.' It wasn't the kind of vibrant, witty chat that I usually go for, but I was still reeling from the discovery that my lovely boyfriend had been exposed to my mother. What had they been talking about? Had they been talking about me? Things could not get any worse.

'So your mum says I can come on your picnic today.'

Which definitely made things worse.

Mum beamed. 'Finn said he'd love to come.'

I shot her a stern look. 'I'm sure you've got other stuff to do,' I said to Finn.

'Nope.'

I was properly panicking by this point. What if he spoke to my dad? How would I stop Sam from doing anything embarrassing? 'I don't mind if you want to go and see Josh,' I said. 'He's probably doing something exciting involving a ball or wheels. Hey, you could play basketball on bikes! That sounds like fun, doesn't it? Call Josh now! Quick!' I attempted to push him towards the door, but he wouldn't move from his stool.

'Honest, Faith,' he said. 'I'm really up for this picnic. We can do that bike-ball thing next week. That way you get to play too.' He grinned as if what I wanted most in the world was to have two Sundays in a row spent doing something stupid.

'Well, that's settled then,' Mum said. 'Who wants to hunt for the frisbee?'

I attempted a smile. Now I know how those people felt on the *Titanic* who bravely played their tubas while the ship went down.

We had to pick up Granny and, as Finn had his bike with him, he said he'd meet us at the woods. This was a good thing because it gave me an opportunity to give my family a friendly pep talk. 'If any of you embarrass me,' I said, 'I will strangle you with your own intestines.'

Granny opened her mouth to say something indignant.

'I've got my eye on you, old lady,' I interrupted. 'You'll keep away from Finn if you know what's good for you. Remember, I've still got photographic evidence of that time you tried to eat my pet rabbit.'

Granny spluttered. 'Really, Faith! I was rubbing noses with him!'

'That's not the way I'll tell it to the RSPCA.'

When we arrived, the wood was as rubbish as ever and the annoying sun had come out quite brightly. Before I had time to lose my family in the trees, Finn came cycling across the car park towards us.

'Is this your little friend?' Granny asked.

I started hoping for rain.

Or an earthquake.

We gathered up all the picnic stuff and once we'd got about three metres from the car park I said, 'This looks like a nice spot,' in such a firm voice that no one argued with me.

Finn was very tolerant of my parents' extreme annoyingness and answered their questions about his family and helped unscrew jars.

When we'd laid all the food out and filled our plates, my dad said, 'So, Finn, what did you think of that Spurs hat-trick?' which was surprising because my dad doesn't like sport.

Finn said, 'Yeah, that was really something. Are you a Spurs supporter, Mr Ashby?'

And the man who once told me that every time you tell a lie one of Santa's elves dies actually said, 'Oh yes, I'm a big fan.'

He's a big something.

I turned my steely gaze on my father. 'What do you think of their chances next weekend?' I asked.

'Well ... on the one hand, they might do well, but then again ... I mean, there's always two sides to every story, aren't there? I think ... that is to say ... It's a game of two halves, isn't it?'

'And how would you say their performance has been this season?'

His old man cheeks started pinking up. 'Oh, you know, much as expected.' He coughed. 'Would you like another sandwich, Finn?'

'Have one of my buns,' Granny said. And she started waving Tupperware in Finn's face.

'Why are you going out with Faith?' Sam asked.

'Sam!' Mum nearly choked on a grape. I don't know why she's surprised that her son has the manners of a rat. I told her this would happen if she didn't beat him.

Lovely Finn wasn't at all bothered. 'I like Faith,' he said to Sam. 'Your sister's cool.'

'No she's not.' Sam went on completely ignoring my death stare and Mum elbowing him in the ribs. 'And if you're good at football couldn't you go out with someone pretty? Or at least nice?'

Mum put a hand over rat boy's mouth. 'That's enough, Sam.'

Finn was actually laughing. 'You're funny! Your kids are really hilarious, Mr Ashby. Sometimes Faith is so funny that she actually makes me cry with laughter.'

'Yes,' said Dad. 'She often brings a tear to my eye.'

At this point Granny obviously felt that she wasn't getting enough attention. 'Oh!' she said. 'Something's tickling in my trousers.'

She honestly did. If the pot of hummus had been deep enough, I would have drowned myself in it.

Mum tried to swat her, but she was still busy keeping Sam's mouth shut.

'No there is,' Granny said. 'I think it's an ant.' She scrambled up, both knees cracking like starter pistols, and began shaking herself about.

I'm telling you now, there was no ant; she just wanted an excuse to wave her geriatric behind in Finn's face. The sight of Granny-bum swinging in the breeze made me think of her prancing with her sweaty, wrinkly bottom in contact with my poor shorts, and the sour-cream dip I'd just eaten started coming back up my throat.

And that was probably the least awful part of the day.

Finally, I convinced everyone that the blue sky might turn to hail at any minute and we packed everything up. I said goodbye to Finn, but it was brief and not romantic. The combination of Granny looking on and the scent of cheese and onion crisps meant that I have never felt less snoggy in my life.

'It's been really good meeting your family,' he said. 'They're cool. We should do it again.'

I practically threw him on to his bike before my mum could whip out her diary and start making dates with my boyfriend.

On the way home Granny said, 'He was a nice boy.'

As if anyone had asked her opinion on my boyfriend.

'But a bit on the flimsy side. Good puff of wind would blow him away.'

Which is ridiculous because you can say what you like about how sport is mind-rottingly boring and on the tiring side, but it does make nice muscles; Finn might be slim, but he is also extremely toned.

'I like some meat on my men,' Granny dribbled on. 'What about that lovely young man I met at the Christmas box thing? You ought to swap that skinny one you've got for him.'

I tried to grapple with the thought that Granny was attempting to send me on a date with Westy, but it was too much for my poor brain and it seized up completely. Fortunately, Granny never minds if you pause in conversation, she just fills the gap.

'And I didn't like those little chocolate cakes we had,' she said. 'You should take them back.'

'We can't,' I said. 'You've eaten them all.'

'I meant you should take back the packet. Get a refund. Or at least a replacement.'

'But you ate them all.'

'Yes, but I hardly enjoyed the last three.'

Needless to say, I won't be taking Granny's advice on exchanging cakes or my boyfriend.

After we'd dropped Granny off, Mum said, 'Well, I don't know about this other boy that Granny was talking about, but I thought Finn was lovely. What a sunny disposition!'

'He'd need one, wouldn't he?' Dad said. 'Dating Faith.' He looked back at me and guffawed. Probably because it's rare that he manages even a sorry attempt at humour like that, so he feels the need to congratulate himself. I gave him the look I usually reserve for Icky. He stared hard at Mum's hands on the steering wheel and said, 'What I mean is, he seems a very pleasant young man. Healthy. Polite.'

'Who were you expecting me to date? A surly vampire?'

Their silence spoke volumes.

LATER

I'm quite put out. Is there anything more annoying that having a boyfriend and parents who really like each other? Surely Finn could have wound them up a little bit if he'd tried? I wonder if he'd consider getting a motorbike.

MONDAY 12TH MARCH

I snuck into town with Megs at lunch today so that she could see Cameron. When we got there, I found that Ethan was with Cam. I haven't spoken to him much since his extreme weirdness at my party, which Megs knows all about, so I wasn't exactly thrilled when she inconsiderately launched into a very long snog with Cam and I was left looking at my feet. You'd think that Ethan would feel a bit embarrassed about his terrible behaviour, but he seemed to have forgotten all about it.

He nodded his head in the direction of the four-armed snog-monster. 'Shame they can't do a GCSE in that, isn't it?'

He's barely acknowledged my presence at debating and I wasn't prepared to just pretend everything was fine. 'Megan is perfectly capable of getting good grades in more traditional subjects,' I said in a stiff voice.

'Cam would be better off with really traditional subjects. Like making a fire and killing stuff with a stick.'

'That's a nice way to talk about your friend.'

Ethan shrugged. 'It's nothing I wouldn't say to his face. Cam is honest about the fact that he's better with his hands than his head. That's one of the things I like about him. He doesn't pretend to be something he's not.'

'What is that supposed to mean?' I asked.

'Nothing.'

We went on like that for the entire duration of Megs and Cam's twenty-minute snogathon. Sometimes Ethan would say something so sarky that I couldn't help laughing, but as chats go it was pretty uncomfortable and tense.

When Megs unglued herself from Cam's face, and the boys left, I let out a long sigh.

'You've got a boyfriend,' Megs said.

'I'm perfectly aware of that.'

'So stop dribbling over Ethan.'

'I am *not* dribbling over him! He drives me mad. He's so rude and infuriating. One minute he's all jokes and the next he's criticising me. That's why I like Finn. He's so simple and straightforward. I mean, not simple like stupid, although I know he's not exactly a genius, but he's just, well, like I said, straightforward.' I was rambling a bit.

Megs gave me a sideways look. 'You are happy with Finn, aren't you?'

I hesitated. 'Well . . .'

'Oh no.'

'Oh no, what?'

Megs threw up her hands. 'This is just like that time you wanted that red dress. You wanted it so much and you kept going on about how it was the loveliest thing you'd ever seen. We had to go and spy on it to make sure no one else was going to get their grubby hands on it while you saved up, and then you finally bought it and you were so pleased with it for about a week, and then you put it on to go to Zoe's party and you stood in front of the mirror and you pulled the exact face that you're pulling now, and I said, "Do you like it?" and you said, "Well . . .".' Finally, she drew breath.

I patted her arm. 'It's nice that you remember the precious times we spend together in such detail, Megs, but I'm not sure that your babbling has got anything to do with the matter in hand.'

'It has! It has!' she started shrieking. She was so shrill she sounded like Icky with a firework in her pants.

'Why has it?'

'Because this is what you do. You want

something and then when you get it you don't want it any more.'

I gave her a stern look. 'If that was true, I wouldn't still be friends with you, screamy lady.'

'You know what I mean!'

'Listen, Megs, the thing is that once I tried that red dress on I realised that it didn't suit me.'

'Are you saying that Finn clashes with your hair?'

'No! I just think we're a bit different. We're not into the same stuff. We don't think the same way.'

'Don't you like him any more?'

'I do like him. Finn's lovely. He really is.' I nearly pretended everything was fine again. But to be honest I'm not used to keeping anything from Megs so I said, 'He's just a bit ...'

'Slow?'

'He's not slow! He's laid-back. I just wish that he ...'

'Didn't say "dude" all the time?'

'I don't mind that. Makes me think I'm in America. I feel quite cheerful when I'm imagining I'm in America.' I blew out a puff of air. 'I don't know. I like Finn. He's nice. I just expected that when I finally got a boyfriend there'd be a bit more to it than talking about crisps.'

'You love snack chat.'

'Yes, but not all the time. I imagined some

227

romance, some laughs and a bit of intellectual discussion.'

Megs stopped and turned to face me. 'Really? Seriously? You imagined intellectual discussions with Finn? Strange and unlikely things happen in your imagination, Faith.'

I let the conversation drop. Anyway, relationships grow and develop, don't they? I'm sure everything will be fine with Finn.

TUESDAY 13TH MARCH

Right now, Finn and I are supposed to be rehearsing our debate, but this afternoon, while Megs and I were at Skye's house running around after Toady, I got a text from Finn. He said, **Hey, Josh got me invited to an indoor rock-climbing party! We can do that speech thing soon.**

What the hell? Does he even realise how soon 'that speech thing' is? We've got to stand up in front of a room full of people and do it the day after tomorrow. Why does my boyfriend think that clambering up some plastic rocks, when there are perfectly good stairs available, is more important than helping me win my bet with Icky?

I am seriously annoyed.

Poor Megs had to listen to me ranting and I'm afraid that I was a bit snappy with Toady too. When he asked me if I had any sweets, I said, 'Do you want all your teeth to turn black and fall out of your head?'

Fortunately, Toady seemed to think that would be hilarious, but Megs said, 'Steady on, Faith. I thought you said that you have to be positive with small children.'

I scowled. 'Yeah, I think my mother may have been whispering hippy thoughts to me as I slept. I've changed my mind. Tough love, Megs, that's the only way to ensure that Toady doesn't end up in prison.'

'Prison? He's not three yet.'

'Refusing Brussel sprouts at three. Truancy at six. Knife crime at nine. We've got to protect this boy.'

If nothing else, Toady enjoyed me stomping about the house. He put on Skye's Doc Martin boots and copied me.

WEDNESDAY 14TH MARCH

I am still cross with Finn. He totally ditched me last night. I have tried to appreciate our differing views and complementary skills, but I just don't understand him. He clearly doesn't understand me either. He sent me a picture of him hanging off the stupid climbing wall. I hardly even noticed how gorgeous he looks in it. There is nothing more cross-making than the person you are cross with not even noticing you are cross. It's our debate tomorrow. Finn had better have a good speech ready.

THURSDAY 15TH MARCH

I am not happy. I am not happy at all. This should have been a brilliant day where I impressed everyone with my amazing debating skills (and made Icky look like the loser she is), but instead I am so angry and sad that I've barely touched this second packet of HobNobs.

Three minutes after the last bell rang I was sitting in debating headquarters (Mrs Lloyd-Winterson's room) totally prepared and looking utterly irresistible. When the boys arrived ten minutes later, my boyfriend was not with them.

'Where's Finn?' I asked Westy.

'Dunno,' he said, pulling a rather crushed piece of banoffee pie wrapped in a napkin out of his pocket.

'Didn't he walk over with the rest of you?'

Westy put half of the pie in his mouth in one go, sending crumbs flying. He shook his head and swallowed. 'We don't exactly hold hands and walk in a crocodile. He's probably here somewhere.'

But Finn isn't the kind of person that you lose track of in a room. He wasn't there and I was starting to panic.

'Don't worry, Faith,' Westy said. 'You don't need him to win a fight.'

I scowled. 'Of course I don't, but that's not the point.'

Westy offered me the other half of his pie, but I declined. I could feel Icky's eyes on me. I knew she'd be delighted if Finn didn't turn up.

She oozed her way over as I was hissing to Megs, 'I'll look like an idiot if I have to go up there by myself.'

'You look like an idiot anyway,' Icky said. 'Don't forget our bet.' And she waggled one of her revolting trotters at me.

Before I could snap her spindly ankle, Ethan appeared beside me. He pretended to elbow Icky in the stomach and then swung up the fist of the same arm as if he was going to smack her in the mouth, but actually he just left his hand a few centimetres from her face, blocking her smarmy chops from my sight. Which was considerate. I don't really want Ethan to do me any favours, but it was nice to hear Icky squealing.

She said, 'Get your filthy hands away from me!' and tried to step past him.

Without acknowledging her, Ethan stepped in front of Icky again, obscuring my view of her malevolent pixie face once more.

'Listen,' Ethan said to me in a low voice. 'If he doesn't show, I'll take his place if you like.'

I was not expecting that. Things have been so

funny between us recently that I was starting to think that Ethan really didn't like me. Half of me wanted to say I didn't need his help, but the other half was so relieved that I said, 'Are you sure? You haven't practised.'

He flashed me a smile. A proper one. It's been a while since he's done that. 'I'll make it up as I go along,' he said. 'It's what I usually do when I speak.'

I was so happy that I wouldn't have to go up there alone that I just nodded.

'You should probably remind me what we're talking about though,' he said.

'It's "Nurses should be paid more than footballers". We're opposing.'

His forehead creased and I could see that he was making rapid plans about what he was going to say. There's no denying that Ethan is pretty quick. And he does know how to talk circles round most people.

'Got it,' he said.

And I knew he had.

'Phew,' Megs said. 'That was lucky.'

But I didn't feel very lucky. I just felt furious. Miss Ramsbottom chose this moment to stalk in through the door and give me a pointed look before sitting down. I wanted to kill Finn. I really needed the debate to go well in front of Miss R, so that she'd give me a good report.

Mrs Lloyd-Winterson clapped her hands for quiet and called the debaters up to the front. Ethan gave my arm a reassuring squeeze. How does he manage to be such a confusing blend of rude and nice? I tried to ignore Icky's smug looks and to get my rage under control. Before I knew it, Mrs L-W was introducing me.

Miss Ramsbottom's beady eyes were fixed on me. Icky was on perma-sneer. But it takes more than the scorn of a vampire lady or the poor punctuality of a surfer to stop me from talking a good talk, so I took a deep breath and launched into my hilarious and deeply convincing speech. I was halfway through explaining why you can't put a price on the national pride footballers stir up, not to mention the laughs we get from their girlfriends' outfits, when the door opened and Finn slipped in. It almost completely put me off. Where the monkey had he been?

Fortunately, at that point, I caught sight of Icky's gloating face. There's nothing like the fuel of hatred to power you through something, so I swept the audience along with me to the triumphant end. There was a lot of clapping. While some people (mostly Westy) were making whooping noises, Finn and Ethan swapped places. I was so cross that I wished Finn hadn't even bothered to turn up.

It was Icky's turn to speak. She made some OK

points, but she had the easy side of the argument and personally I found it hard to concentrate with her shrill voice squeaking away. She kept throwing her scrawny little arms out, which I think was supposed to emphasise what she was saying, but she nearly had her teammate's eye out with her nails at least twice.

Then it was Finn. He was pretty bad. I suppose I should be grateful that he took my hints to heart, but I hadn't really intended for him to just read them out as a list. At the end he said, 'This is so important. Footballers and nurses both do brilliant jobs.' Which suggests that he didn't really understand what it was that he was arguing for in the first place.

Icky's teammate was good. He spoke clearly and made sense and didn't employ any dangerous arm movements. When it was all over, I felt that Icky's team had been consistently competent, whereas on my side I had been brilliant, but Finn was lame. I honestly didn't know how it was going to go. I held my breath during the voting. When the hands were up for my team, I could see that it was close, but even as Mrs Lloyd-Winterson was saying, 'You can only vote with one hand, young man,' to Westy, I knew we'd lost.

Mrs Lloyd-Winterson drew things to a close and I really wanted to get out of there as quickly as possible. I didn't want to talk to Finn, I didn't want to hear Miss Ramsbottom's verdict and I definitely didn't want Icky telling me to kiss her feet. Unfortunately, we were on the far side of the classroom and there was a bit of a jam at the door. I busied myself with my bag and said to Megs under my breath, 'Just keep talking to me. I don't want to talk to anyone else.'

Megs looked at me with an open mouth, which is ridiculous because ordinarily I can't get her to shut up.

'Erm ...' she said. 'I thought you were very good.'

'Not about the debate. Anything else but that.'

She scrunched her face in concentration. 'Mrs L-W is completely taking up Miss Ramsbottom's attention with some exciting chat, probably about chin-hair removal, which neither of them are skilled at. If we're quick, we might get out without Miss R cornering you.'

I looked up at the teachers and saw Finn coming towards us; before he reached me, Ethan tapped him on the shoulder and said, 'You should have been here.'

Even though Ethan said it in quite an unpleasant tone, Finn smiled at him and said, 'Yeah, thanks for covering for me, bro.'

Ethan stiffened. 'I'm not your bro; I would

have thought that it was obvious from my superior genetic make-up that we are in no way related, and I didn't cover for you, I covered for Faith. Because you stuffed up.'

Finn blinked a bit at that.

Who does Ethan think he is? What business was it of his? 'Leave it, Ethan,' I said.

Ethan looked at me. His shoulders were tensed up. 'I'm just saying that the least he could manage is attendance; no one was expecting him to contribute much else.'

Just because he's clever he thinks that he can tell everyone what he thinks of them. He's so arrogant. 'Stop it!' I snapped. 'Stop being horrible to Finn.'

Ethan's face hardened. 'Oh, come on, Faith, he would have to understand what I'm saying to be insulted.'

Finn looked between us. He obviously didn't know what to say. 'Sorry I was late?' he hazarded. It was clear that Ethan was right and that Finn didn't really know what was going on.

'Just forget it,' I said. 'It's all fine.' And I stalked out of the classroom with my head high.

Then I had to walk back in again to pick up my bag and a gawping Megs.

LATER

I'm furious. I know I sound like I'm having a

tantrum just because I didn't win, but that's not really why I'm so upset. I can't believe that Ethan did that. As if things weren't bad enough. Why did he have to draw more attention to the fact my boyfriend let me down? Sometimes I think he likes watching things go wrong for me.

As for Finn, it was really important to me to win that bet, but he just didn't care. He didn't want to practise; he didn't want to turn up. He'd rather be climbing walls or surfing, or anything where he doesn't have to think or disagree with anyone.

LATER STILL

And the person that I'm crossest with is myself because I've known that about him all along and have just been kidding myself that things were fine.

LATEREST

And what am I supposed to do about Icky's feet?

FRIDAY 16TH MARCH

What a rubbish day. I'm still angry. Miss Ramsbottom spoke to me at registration.

'You performed well yesterday, Faith.'

There was a pause here where I think she expected me to be all super grateful, but I wasn't in the mood to pretend to be paying her attention.

'It's nice to see you applying yourself to something worthwhile,' she said. 'I look forward to seeing more from the debating club. Although next time you might want to reconsider your choice of partner. He was woefully underprepared.'

I ignored that and asked, 'Does this mean that I'll get a good report?'

'If you keep up the hard work and good behaviour for the rest of the term.'

Honestly. What a con. You behave well for adults once and they just keep wanting more. They're never satisfied.

On top of Miss R's insatiable appetite for unrealistically perfect conduct, I had to put up with Icky popping up and asking, 'When are you going to kiss my feet?'

'Fine,' I said, 'let's get it over with.'

'Not here. I want a big audience.' She contorted her face in a horrible way, which I assume meant she was thinking. 'Save it for the next party so I can really enjoy your humiliation.'

I gave her my daggers look.

She just sniffed. 'I'd have thought you'd be good at arguing, Faith, what with your gigantic gob.'

So I said, 'Whereas no one expects you to be good at anything, Vicky, what with you being a gigantic idiot.'

It's unfortunate that Mrs Baxter happened to overhear that last remark. 'Faith!' she snapped. 'Don't insult your classmates.'

So the next time I called Icky a gigantic something I whispered it.

Then I had to suffer assembly with the blank-faced Student Council. They were going on about their stupid suggestion box again. They said they were looking for ideas to combat bullying. Well, you know me; I always like to help, or at the very least say what I think, so I popped in a new suggestion. It said, 'Sack Miss Ramsbottom.' That should wipe out about 95 per cent of the bullying in this school.

SATURDAY 17TH MARCH

I went shopping with the girls today. Angharad was shining like a sunbeam when she opened the door to me this morning.

'What is it?' I asked.

'It's Elliot!'

'Have you two kissed?' I could hardly begin to imagine how incredibly cute that would be. Like two little puppies rubbing noses.

'No!' Angharad said. 'No kissing, but he asked Cam to ask Megs to find out if I wanted to meet up to sort out our debate!'

That is practically a marriage proposal

considering how slow those two are. I am so pleased for her.

But I'm not sure that a shopping trip with three loved-up friends was the best place for me today.

I need to see Finn to sort things out. I've arranged to meet him tomorrow.

SUNDAY 18TH MARCH

Urgh. Part of me hoped that when I saw Finn today it would be awful and that we'd have a row and that my mind would be made up about him, but he was exactly the same as usual. He apologised about the debate, even though it's obvious that he doesn't understand why it's a big deal. He was sweet and spacey, just like he was on our first date. But something has changed. I think it's the way that I look at him. I could forgive him for letting me down, but the whole thing has made me realise that I can't ignore the fact that Finn and I are very different and I don't just mean we're not into the same things. We *feel* differently about stuff.

Also, while I can't deny that he is still lovely to look at, and the one go at snogging that we had then wasn't exactly unpleasant, he doesn't give me tingles any more.

I didn't know what to say to him or what to do. It was a very quiet date. I'm starting to wonder if maybe it was me doing most of the chatting anyway.

MONDAY 19TH MARCH

I'm miserable. I have been miserable all day. At lunchtime I only had to do a little bit of rolling about and sighing before my so-called friends noticed I was not happy.

'What's the matter, Faith?' Lily said finally.

'She's gone off Finn,' Megs said in an entirely unsympathetic fashion.

'Have you?' Ang asked.

Lily gasped. 'Did he do something horrible?'

'No! Not at all. Finn is never horrible to anyone. And that's part of the problem. You know how much I enjoy stinging people with my acerbic wit?'

'She means being mean to people,' Ang explained to Lily.

'Well, Finn is not as keen,' I said. 'He just smiles at everyone. He's just so *nice*.'

'I thought you liked him being nice and sweet and cheerful and all that,' Lily said.

'I do. He's lovely. But he's not ...'

Megs gave me a significant look and I knew she was about to say 'Ethan' so I quickly said, 'He's not right for me.'

Ang looked like I'd just said I'd stopped believing in Santa. 'I thought he made you feel all tingly.'

'He did. But he doesn't any more.'

Lily looked solemn. 'Your love has died,' she said in her funeral voice.

I burst out laughing. 'I don't think it ever really got to that stage,' I said. 'We were only official for seven and a half weeks.'

The girls exchanged glances. 'You do realise that you're talking about your relationship with Finn in the past tense, don't you?' Meg asked.

I half shrugged.

'Does that mean it's all over?' Lily asked.

I think it does.

LATER

It's a bit strange. This time last week I didn't even want to admit there was a problem. Now I seem to have decided to finish things all of a sudden. If I'm honest with myself, I suppose things have been building up. I feel sad.

TUESDAY 20TH MARCH

I arranged to meet Finn after babysitting.

I was actually quite happy to see Toady. At least he's never let me down. He is reliably grumpy and screechy every time I see him. Megs had a date with Cameron so it was just me and Toady today. We had a pretty good time with the Play-Doh. Toady's creations mostly looked like splats of goulash, but I was pleased with my sculpture of a beautiful but sad girl which I called 'the end of the relationship'. I showed it to

Toady; he clapped his hands in appreciation of my skill.

And then he reached out a chubby fist and squished it flat.

'Yeah,' I said. 'That's pretty much how I feel.'

Toad beamed up at me.

'Listen,' I said, making him a Play-Doh pizza. 'When you're older, don't bother with this dating business. It just makes you feel rubbish in the end.'

Toady nodded his head, snatched the Play-Doh pizza out of my hand and took a large bite.

By the time I got to Juicy Lucy's, I was already quite tired from wrestling with Toad to get the Play-Doh out of his hair and just the thought of having to have a big conversation with Finn sent a wave of exhaustion through me. When Finn arrived (ten minutes late), he gave me a gleaming grin and I wondered if he'd even noticed that things haven't exactly been great recently.

I let him chat a bit and then I had to say, 'Listen, Finn, I think we need to talk.'

'Yeah?' He was still smiling.

'The thing is, Finn, we're quite different. I mean, I like sitting down and being the best at stuff and having blood feuds with annoying people, and you ...'

'I like surfing.'

'Mmm-hmm, you do. Which is fine. I like

the beach. Of course, I don't like sand in my sandwiches, or when you find a dead crab, or getting changed under a towel.'

'The beach is pretty cool.'

If I'd let him get started on a list of what he thinks is pretty cool, we'd have been there all night.

'I just think that we're maybe not a good match,' I blurted out.

He nodded his head slowly.

'So maybe we should, you know, just be friends.'

'Yeah, you're a good friend, Faith.'

Which made me wonder if we'd ever really been dating. But I definitely remember some snogging.

'So . . . we'll just call it a day on the, er, well, the kissing and that.'

'I liked the kissing.' And he gave me such an impish grin that the reasons I liked him in the first place came flooding back to me.

Then I remembered the debating fiasco. 'We're not suited,' I said firmly. 'It's better if we're just friends.'

He nodded slowly. 'OK.'

OK? OK? This must be the worst break-up in the history of ever. I was expecting it to be hard because Finn was going to be all upset and possibly a little bit teary because he could hardly bear the thought of life without me, and there he was saying 'OK' as if it didn't really bother him.

He stood up. 'We've had some fun times, Faith. I guess I'll see you around.'

And then, just to show that there were no hard feelings, he gave me this little peck on the cheek. *How dare he?* How dare he have no hard feelings? Why was he not weeping on my shoulder? This is not how my spurned lovers are supposed to behave.

LATER

He hasn't even sent me any texts begging me to take him back. Surely he should be serenading me outside my window by now?

LATER STILL

Nothing from Finn. I'm starting to suspect that he won't even bother to have me followed by a private detective.

I am devastated.

WEDNESDAY 21ST MARCH

I banned everyone from talking about Finn today. This didn't stop Icky from slinking past me and the girls, saying, 'I might date a blond next, maybe a surfer type,' to her stupid friends.

She's lucky I painted my nails yesterday so I

didn't want them to get mucky with her eyeball gloop.

I told Mum about it this evening. I said, 'Icky will probably convince Finn to go out with her somehow. She's had tons of boyfriends and no one can understand why.'

Mum frowned. 'I don't think you should be criticising her for her, erm, healthy appetites. You know I hate to see double standards when people talk about dating.'

'It's not the number of boyfriends I'm criticising. There's a girl in Year Eleven called Fi Wilkins who has dated a gazillion boys. She's our idol. The thing that I'm criticising about Icky is, well, pretty much everything, but mostly the fact that she seems to enjoy other people's misery and she's rubbing in me breaking up with Finn and she won't even wait to pounce on him. Other girls would allow a respectable period of mourning of two to four weeks.'

'I see. How will you feel if Finn does date someone else?'

I pouted. 'I suppose it's unreasonable to expect him to sit alone in a stone tower clutching a lock of my hair and whispering my name?'

Mum nodded.

'Then I guess I'll learn to live with it.'

'You'll be dating again soon too.' She gave me a hug. 'In the mean time I want you to remember that you're very special and you deserve someone just as special.'

As you know, I have always considered my mother to be a very wise lady.

THURSDAY 22ND MARCH

Finn didn't come to debating club today. I would like to think that this is because he's discovered that he actually is heartbroken and that he thinks, if he sees my face, he'll break down and sob, but I suspect that really it's because he was never that keen on debating in the first place.

It's probably best that we have split up. What kind of person doesn't enjoy a good argument?

Although it's best to win arguments and then you don't get stuck doing stupid forfeits like kissing Icky's troll toes. While I was waiting for Mum to pick me up from debating, Icky came tripping over and said, 'Everyone's going to Juicy Lucy's at the end of term. You can keep your promise to kiss my feet there.'

I didn't answer. I don't back out of bets, but no one said anything about it being with an audience. I think I might spring a surprise attack on Icky's witch feet, then I'll have kept my side of the bet without her making me look like an idiot.

'Hope Finn gets to see you kissing up to my tootsies,' she said. 'I'm not surprised he came to his senses and dumped you. I heard you begged him to take you back.'

'You heard wrong,' I snapped. 'Might be something to do with your misshapen ears.'

She pulled her innocent face. Which is a lot like a cat with a dead mouse in its paw. 'Haven't you split up then?'

I looked down my nose at her. 'We may have parted ways, but it was me who decided it was over.'

Icky laughed. 'Yeah, right!'

I turned and walked towards the gates.

'That's it, walk away from the truth!' Icky called.

I turned back. 'Oh, I'm not walking away, you simpering leprechaun,' I said. 'I'm taking a run-up.'

I have to say that, for someone who has never received any formal tuition in the martial arts, I've got some nice moves.

LATER

Ethan wasn't at debating club either. Which is a bit rich given that he lectured Finn about the importance of attendance.

I didn't want to see him anyway.

FRIDAY 23RD MARCH

I do know that there's no point in hanging on to a boyfriend who's not right for you. I do know that one day I will have a brilliant relationship with someone who makes me melt and also understands my sense of humour.

But none of this helps with the fact that all my friends are out with their boyfriends.

And I am here.

Alone.

SATURDAY 24TH MARCH

The girls and I went to the cinema today and afterwards we had pizza. When we were sitting at the table with Lily rabbiting on about how to avoid paradoxes when time-travelling, and Angharad doing a sum on a napkin using pi to work out what the best value pizza was, Megs reached across and gave my hand a squeeze to make sure I was OK, but I totally was. Sometimes it's nice just to be with the girls. We didn't talk about boys at all. I love my friends.

Mum is still being really nice. This evening she made me a cup of tea and patted me on the head. She said, 'Would you like some of my special chocolate?'

'Do you mean the good kind of special or the special kind of special?'

Mum tutted. 'I mean that it's organic with 75 per cent cocoa solids and slivers of ginger root in it. It's delicious.'

'That stuff that looks like lumps of mud with bits of twig in? No thanks. But if sympathy chocolate is available I will take a couple of Dad's Snickers.'

'All right,' Mum said and pulled one out of the cupboard. (Just one. I've noticed she's got selective hearing when it comes to quantities – she only ever makes me two pieces of toast even when I've requested six or eight.) She ruffled my hair. 'I'm glad you're not letting a boy diminish your appetite for chocolate. I hope that the same thing is true of your appetite for life and your thirst for fulfilment.'

I burst out laughing. 'Mum, if I ever do get really depressed, you should just give me a two-minute blast of your hippy talk. If that doesn't crack me up, nothing will.'

Mum shook her head. 'I don't have to use my philosophy on life to make you laugh, young lady.' She flexed her fingers at me.

'No! Not the tickling.' I held up my almost finished cup of tea 'I'm holding hot liquid! Health and safety! Health and safety!'

But she reached behind me and pulled the cup out of my hand and laid in with a tickle attack that could have taken down several marines. I'm telling you, I'm sure the only reason she does yoga is so that she's flexible enough to pin me to the floor with one elbow and a couple of toes, to leave her hands free for torture tickling.

When I'd finally managed to get out a dignified request for her to cease and desist ('Mum! Mum! Pleeeeeeease stop it!'), we both collapsed on the sofa for a rest.

'So you're all right then?' she asked.

'Yeah. I mean I feel a bit ...' I blew out a big breath. 'A bit flat. But I think Finn and I are probably better suited as friends.'

'That sounds very wise and mature, Faith. Do you know there's a women's group that believe—'

But I silenced her by wisely and maturely putting a cushion over her head.

SUNDAY 25TH MARCH

Granny came round today to 'look after' me and Sam while my feckless parents went to some elderly person's fortieth birthday party.

I said to Dad, 'I don't need looking after. And who has a birthday party at lunchtime? Is that so that all you old folk are back home in time for the rubbish Sunday night telly?'

'Sam needs looking after,' Dad insisted.

'I could do that. You lock him in his room and I promise not to forget to throw him something to eat.'

My parents always say that they're open to sensible suggestions, but Dad completely ignored that one.

After they'd gone, I worked my way through a bag of doughnuts while Granny faffed about, tidying up and listening to Radio Four and other pointless stuff like that.

MONDAY 26TH MARCH

I did tell my parents that Granny shouldn't be in the house unsupervised, but they never listen. Earlier, Granny came round with one of her boyfriends (Jim, who Granny says 'made a lot of money in tights' – I can only hope that he was selling the tights rather than earning cash while wearing them). Anyway, Granny opened up the cupboard under the stairs and started handing Jim a load of black bin bags, all bulging suspiciously.

'What have you got in there?' I asked.

'Just a few things I tidied up yesterday,' Granny said.

I haven't forgotten her shorts theft. 'Let me see,' I said.

Sure enough, the crafty old biddy had seven bin bags crammed full of our stuff. She had half my shoe collection and all of my stuffed animals.

'Mum!' I screeched. 'Granny's stealing from us again!'

'Again?' Jim asked. He was starting to look a bit uncomfortable.

'It was a misunderstanding about some silver spoons,' Granny said.

'Yeah,' I said. 'Granny misunderstood when Mum said she wasn't allowed to steal them.'

Granny started wittering on about how she was collecting for a jumble sale and it was all for a very good cause. And she'd packed these things up when she was here yesterday and no one had even noticed. Fortunately, Mum's growling abilities came to the fore and we got back all our stuff.

I actually felt a bit sorry for Granny in the end so, when she and Jim were leaving, I slipped her the bag with Mum's dreamcatcher collection in. 'And you can have these.' I handed her a horrible pair of bunny slippers that I've never taken the tags off. The rabbits look like they've got myxomatosis.

Granny's smile faded. 'I gave you those,' she snapped.

I didn't let my smile slip. 'Yes,' I said, 'and isn't it wonderful to think of someone else owning them and getting to experience the same joy that I did?'

She poked me in the neck with her umbrella.

That's what you get for being charitable.

TUESDAY 27TH MARCH

Megs was meeting Cam in the park after school today. Since it's sort of on the way to Skye's house,

I walked with her. But when we got there he had Ethan with him.

'Did you know he'd be here?' I hissed to Megs.

Megs didn't answer, which is a clear admission of guilt to me.

Ethan was looking at me with his big dark eyes. He said, 'Hi.'

I said, 'Hi,' back, but I think it was obvious that I didn't mean it. I turned round to leave.

'Faith! Wait a minute,' Ethan said.

'I've got a job to go to,' I said. 'I'll be late.'

Megs and Cam were drifting away to give us some privacy, even though I was giving Megs a look that clearly said that I didn't want any.

'What is it?' I asked Ethan.

He looked a bit uncomfortable, which is a first for Ethan.

'Look, I'm sorry if I interfered at debating club.' He said it in a rush. It was obviously hard for him to get the words out.

'OK,' I said.

There was a pause.

I remembered how relieved I was when he offered to take Finn's place. 'It was nice of you to say that you'd do the speech at the last minute,' I said in a stilted voice.

'Wow,' said Cam. 'Steady on, you two. Any more of your sweet talking and I'll be sick.'

Everybody laughed.

Ethan and I sat on the swings for a bit.

'Listen,' he said, 'I've always found myself to be delightful company, but apparently I can be a bit of an idiot sometimes, so if there's anything else that I've done or said that's upset you ...' He looked right into my eyes and I couldn't help thinking about that time I thought he was going to kiss me and I wondered if he was thinking about it too.

'... Then I'm sorry about that too.'

It wasn't a very specific apology, but at least it shows that he realises he's been a bit mean to me recently.

'I assume that there's some sort of cash compensation,' I said.

'As soon as I win my court case against my History teacher for defamation, I'll give you a cut.'

'I think I'd get a better deal if I fine you a pound every time you say something sarcastic.'

'Oh, that's a *marvellous* idea.'

'I'll put that on your tab.'

I wanted to hang around joking with him, but I really did have to get to Skye's.

I'm pleased that things are better with Ethan.

LATER

When I got home this evening, Mum asked me how babysitting went. I said, 'Do you know? I quite like Toad now. In a way. I think I'll keep up the babysitting even though I'm not so desperate for the money any more.' Then I realised that actually I never did get round to mentioning that holiday I was planning to take with Finn, so I quickly went on. 'And I've come round to your way of parenting.'

Mum smiled. 'You mean you managed to create a loving, supportive environment with the freedom for self-expression?'

I snorted. 'No, I mean I put his snack on a tray and turned on the TV.' I gave her a suspicious look. 'And what was that freedom stuff you were talking about? That wasn't my childhood.'

'Yes it was!' She pushed her straggling locks out of her face. 'Well, that was always my intention. If I didn't quite succeed, it was probably because you were a difficult child.'

'Definitely didn't happen to me. Probably something you read in a book,' I said.

'I did try to give you creative opportunities—'

'Or a film you saw.'

Mum frowned. 'Stop ignoring me! I'm just saying that I've certainly always been supportive.'

'A dream? Did you dream it?'

'Faith, I don't think that's very funny. I did my best.'

'Perhaps one of your mad friends told you about it?'

At that point she left the room. She even slammed the door a bit. Old people are so immature.

THURSDAY 29TH MARCH

Today it was Westy and his partner Mei's turn to debate. They were arguing that we should be able to leave school at fifteen.

When the boys arrived, Westy was looking pretty sick. He faffed about pulling everything out of his pockets. 'I've lost the last page of my notes!' he said to me. 'I can't do it without my notes!'

I helped him sift through the bus tickets and chocolate wrappers from his pockets. 'Don't start panicking, Westy,' I said in a helpful way.

'I'm not starting,' he said, tugging his tie. 'I've been panicking for weeks.'

We found the screwed-up little bit of paper he was looking for, but actually he didn't really need it because, once he got going, Westy didn't stop for anything. His style of debating is pretty much the same as his approach to everyday conversation, i.e. loud. You could tell which points he thought were particularly brilliant because he repeated them at an even higher volume. But he was definitely enthusiastic, which must count for a lot because they won. When Mrs L-W announced it, Westy lifted Mei off her feet and she squealed. I was really pleased for them.

When we were all hanging about at the gates, Ethan said, 'Hey Faith, you did a good job organising this debating thing.'

Which surprised me because Ethan doesn't praise people very often.

'Well, you know me, I'm always trying to give young people opportunities to get together and be outshone by my linguistic skills.'

He smiled. 'You are very good at talking. It's one of my favourite things about you.'

I really wanted to ask him what the other things were, but someone yelled, 'Ethan! You walking with us, or what?'

I looked up; it was Ryan, he was on the other side of the road with two St Minger's girls. One of them was black-haired Dawn from my party.

'Got to go,' Ethan said. 'Ryan's lending me his amp.'

I just shrugged. He can walk home with whoever he chooses.

Anyway, when I was the last one left waiting for my tardy father, I decided that I wasn't going to think about Ethan or any boy for at least a month. Which was difficult because Icky came skipping over and started singing, 'Finn dumped you because you're so gross.' In my ear.

But I found that the rhythm of me kicking her really took my mind off it.

FRIDAY 30TH MARCH

Tomorrow is Lily's birthday. I am in charge of making the cake for her bowling gathering. When I told Mum this, she started making faces and asked if I'd read the recipe through very carefully. She obviously thinks I'm not capable of baking a cake. I don't know why people make such a fuss about cooking. It's really just stirring and heating.

LATER

I don't know why anyone ever cooks anything ever. It takes a lot of time and effort and in the end you might as well just buy it at Tesco. Except I have spent the cake money on ingredients so Lily will not be getting one of those nice fluffy supermarket cakes with the perfectly smooth icing.

She will be getting my effort.

Which has more of a rustic look.

LATER STILL

I heard Dad go into the kitchen and say, 'Flaming Nora! There's a dead animal in our kitchen!'

I assumed that it was a rat, attracted by my mother's vast supply of beans and grains, but then he said, 'It's crawled on to a plate and died. I think it sneezed its guts up. I've never seen so much slime!' and I knew he was referring to my culinary efforts.

Maybe chocolate cake with green mint icing wasn't such a good combination.

SATURDAY 31ST MARCH

On our way to Lily's gathering Megs said, 'You and Ethan looked very friendly after debating.'

I shrugged. 'Things are still a bit weird between us.'

'Maybe you should unweird them. Then perhaps the rest of us won't have to put up with all this nonsense.'

'What do you mean nonsense?'

'Faith, we all know that you've always had a thing for Ethan.'

'No I haven't! I mean, Ethan is a very clever young man. And he is good-looking. And there is something really appealing about his dark sense of humour ... Oh all right, maybe I have had feelings for Ethan in the past, but recently we haven't been so friendly.'

'Why not?'

'Things aren't quite the same as they were before. I don't think he likes me any more. I think he thinks I'm an idiot for going out with Finn.'

'You are an idiot for going out with Finn, but I don't think that Ethan has gone off you. Anyone who has a strong enough stomach to get keen on you in the first place isn't going to be scared off by your first bit of nonsense.'

'And I've been meaning to tell you what a great girl you are too, Megs.'

'Don't get stroppy; I'm just telling it like it is. You really ought to sort things out with Ethan.'

I wasn't expecting to have a great time bowling, but I decided to make sure that Lily enjoyed herself because that's what counts when you give up on your own happiness and just live for others.

Lily wore a T-shirt with a picture of a dog and a cat getting married. She really doesn't seem to care about looking glamorous around Arif. The general effect of this seems to be that he adores her.

Ethan turned up late. I didn't mean to be pleased to see him, but I really was. I ended up having a lot of fun. I love the way that Ethan and I can build on each other's jokes. It makes me feel smart and funny, and like I'm part of a secret club. I've got to admit that I may have started wondering what it would be like to touch his lovely messy curls, but then Megs spoiled everything by taking a good look at us and saying, 'Why don't you two come out with me and Cam next Saturday?'

Obviously, that was too much because Ethan said, 'Sorry, I'm busy next week.'

And after that he was a lot less chatty.

I could kill Megs.

I didn't do brilliantly at knocking down pins, but fortunately Angharad is a bowling wonder and you can always rely on her to keep the girls' average score up. She was making yet another strike when Megs said, 'Isn't that Icky over there?'

It was. Two lanes over Icky and her gang of brainless followers were posing and shouting and generally bringing down the levels of attractiveness in the place. They were accompanied by about twenty boys. *Twenty boys*. Not only is Icky mean, she's also greedy.

I tried to ignore them, but it was pretty difficult. Icky was strutting about in a pair of bright pink jeans as if she owned the place. She obviously thought that she was important enough to ignore the rules because instead of proper bowling shoes she was wearing a pair of spike heels almost as ugly as the ones she wore to the club night.

I watched Westy dancing about like a ballerina, but still only managing to take down one pin, then I saw the guy from behind the counter tap Icky on the shoulder.

'You can't wear street shoes in this area,' he said.

'It's all right,' Icky said in a stupid throaty voice. 'I'm not bowling.'

'If you're on the lane, you wear the shoes.'

I nudged Megs, but she was already watching. I nudged Lily instead.

'Do I really have to?' Icky simpered. Her whole crowd was watching this exchange and I really think she thought she was going to charm him into letting it go.

'It's the rules.' He was starting to sound seriously annoyed.

Icky batted her eyelashes. 'But you're not wearing bowling shoes.'

'I work here.'

By this point, an awful lot of people had stopped bowling so that they could watch what was going on.

Icky pouted. Things weren't going her way and she didn't like it. 'It doesn't really matter; the floor's all marked anyway. This isn't exactly a world-class bowling alley, is it?'

The guy shook his head in disgust. 'Put the shoes on or leave. Now.'

Icky scowled. 'Fine! I didn't want to stay in this disgusting place anyway.' And she turned her back on him ready to strop off. But she really shouldn't have spun round so hard in shoes with no grip because she lost her footing, staggered backwards with her arms windmilling and landed smack on her behind with her legs in the air.

As Mrs Webber is fond of pointing out, I'm

unable to let the opportunity to say something smart go by so, while other people were sucking in their breath or giggling, I dashed forward and grabbed Icky by the ankle.

I screwed up my face. 'Phew! Don't worry, Vicky, even if you're not wearing bowling shoes, your feet still smell like you are.' That got a loud laugh and while people were clutching at each other I planted a smacker on Icky's foot.

I leant down to her level. 'That's my side of the bet kept. You wanted an audience, you got one.'

She was absolutely seething. I think she'd been hoping for a situation where she wasn't the one who looked like a total idiot, but there was nothing she could do because I had definitely completed my forfeit. Her face turned the same colour as her jeans. I thought her head would go off like a party popper.

Everyone agreed that it rounded off the birthday celebrations nicely.

LATER

I'm really happy about Icky getting what she deserves, but I keep going over my conversations with Ethan. Why did he turn down Megs's suggestion? Is he really busy? Or doesn't he like me? I wish I knew what was going on inside his head.

LATER STILL

No one ate much of the cake except Lily. She said,
'It's like a giant inside-out After Eight. I love it.'

At least I always know what Lily is thinking.

APRIL

SUNDAY 1ST APRIL

Sam wouldn't stop staring at me while I was eating my Coco Pops this morning. 'What is it, you pustule?' I asked.

'I'm ready,' he said.

'Ready for what? Nursery school?'

He folded his arms. 'I haven't forgotten that it's April Fool's day and I'm telling you, you can't trick me.'

'I don't go in for all that April Fool's day stuff. I think it's a bit sad if a sister has to wait for a special day to show her little brother how much she enjoys making him look like a loser. I like to laugh at you every day of the year.'

He narrowed his eyes.

'Seriously,' I said. 'It would be unoriginal and unsatisfying for me to try to trick you today.'

He didn't reply, but I noticed that his shoulders relaxed a little.

Big mistake.

At teatime Sam was left with a plate full of tomato sauce because I'd loosened the top on the squeezy ketchup bottle.

He snarled at me and said, 'I thought you said it would be unoriginal and unsatisfying?'

'Yeah,' I said. 'It is.' I leant back and stretched out my arms and legs in contentment. 'But it's also still really funny.'

MONDAY 2ND APRIL

On Thursday everyone will be in Juicy Lucy's to celebrate the end of term.

'Do you think I should be worried that Icky will try to pay me back in front of an audience?' I asked Megs.

'I heard she's so embarrassed she's going to give it a miss.'

'So who will be there? Is Eth— I mean, are all the boys coming?'

She nodded in an annoyingly knowing way, so I said, 'There'll be loads of boys from Radcliffe there, though, won't there? Probably Year Eleven boys too. I'm thinking that maybe I'd be happier with a more mature boy.'

'Never mind Year Eleven; it's about time you and Ethan got it together.'

'Yeah, just remember what happened the last time you tried to push him into a date with me,' I said. 'He was like a startled rabbit. So keep your nose out. Anyway, I don't even know how I feel about Ethan. He's totally unpredictable and he thinks he's so clever.'

'Sounds like someone else I know.'

I walloped Megs as if I didn't have a care in the world, but I really don't understand Ethan. Sometimes he's all friendly and sometimes he gives me the brush-off.

'Maybe I do like him,' I admitted. 'But I don't like it when he makes me feel like an idiot. I've already got Ramsbottom to do that. And there was all that showing me up when he started pointing out that Finn had let me down.'

Megs folded her arms. 'Has it ever occurred to you that the reason he was so off with Finn is because he likes you?'

'If he liked me, he wouldn't make me feel so stupid for going out with Finn.'

'He would if he'd rather that you were going out with him.'

'He told my boyfriend off right in front of me!'

'Yeah, because he thinks you deserve better. He was thinking about you.'

'If he thinks I'm so great, why did he look horrified when you suggested a double date?'

She didn't have an answer for that one.

I'm confused. I do want Ethan to like me, but do I want a relationship now? What if it all went horribly wrong again? Perhaps I should stick to my plan of giving all this boy stuff a rest for a while.

TUESDAY 3RD APRIL

It was Skye's last class at the community centre today so this is the end of my babysitting for Toad.

I thought we might as well enjoy ourselves so

271

I let Toady have a little bit of everything his mum says he can't have. We started with sugary cereal and moved on to cartoons and electronic toys. By the time Skye came home, he was running round in circles.

'Someone is happy!' Skye said.

'Oh yes,' I said. 'He's bursting with the joy of life.'

Skye asked me to have a cup of tea with her. I nearly told her that I can get twig tea and hippy chat at home, but I suddenly felt strangely reluctant to say goodbye to Toad, so I stayed.

'You've done a great job, Faith,' Skye said. 'I know that Tolde has really benefited from having your young energy in the house. He's going to miss you.'

I was thinking how I'd miss the money, but then Toad held out his pudgy hand to me and when I leant forward to take it he snatched it away and thumbed his nose just like I taught him. That's when I realised that actually I *am* going to miss the little toadling.

When I finally left, Skye tried to pick Toad up, but he arched his back and threw his arms about so she had to put him down. Then he flung his arms round my legs. I bit my lip.

'Do you think maybe I could come and visit Toa— I mean Tolde sometimes?' I asked.

'Of course. I was going to ask if maybe you could babysit in the evenings occasionally?'

I nodded. A lot. It's funny how stuff you really don't want to do can end up being enjoyable.

I had to go before I started snivelling. I patted Toad's head. 'Bye-bye then, Tolde.' I bent down and whispered in his ear. 'Don't forget what I told you. You can achieve anything if you whine hard enough to get someone else to do it for you.'

WEDNESDAY 4TH APRIL

I've found myself thinking about Ethan all day. He really is very funny. And fit. And maybe Megs is right about him fancying me because things between us have definitely been more charged this year. In fact, he's only really been weird since I started dating Finn. I just don't know what to do.

Normally, I'm a very decisive person, but last night Mum offered me the choice between her vegetable moussaka and her vegetable crumble (I have mentioned that maybe one day we could go crazy and eat something that isn't made entirely of vegetables). I found myself in a strange position: I didn't know which to choose.

Mum said, 'Come on, which is it?'

'I don't know. I mean, I think I like crumble at the moment, but what if I choose it and then later on I realise that I'm not so keen? Will I still get to be friends with the crumble?'

Mum looked at me. 'We're not talking about my cooking here any more, are we?'

I shook my head. 'Although, before we move on, I'd like to suggest that we explore a third way and go for chips. Which, if you think about it, is about as much pure vegetable composition as you can get.'

Mum screwed up her nose. 'Never mind your love of greasy food. Do you want to tell me what you're worrying about?'

I sighed. 'I'm trying to decide how much I like a boy. And, if I really do like him, is it a good idea for me to do anything about it?'

Mum pulled her sympathetic face. It's similar to her trapped-wind face. 'That's a tough decision, but I can't tell you what to do, my sweet.'

I nearly fell off my chair. 'What do you mean? You're always telling me what to do. Finish your homework ... No, you can't make home-made explosives ... Stop strangling your brother. It's an endless list of commands from you.'

'I just mean that you have to follow your heart.'

'Are you sure about that? My heart hasn't got a great track record. Remember that time I dropped my Benny Bear in the swimming pool and I jumped in after him even though I couldn't swim? It was my heart that told me to do that. Also, that time I lay down in front of the car of that primary school teacher I didn't want to leave, and when I tried to give Megs and me matching neck tattoos. They all came from my heart.'

'Hmm. But you're older and wiser now. This is a bit different.'

'Yeah, I just don't want Ethan to turn out to be a red dress or a soggy teddy bear.'

Mum looked confused. 'All I can say is that when it comes to relationships no one really knows whether things will work out, but sometimes you like someone so much that you're prepared to take the risk of getting hurt.'

Which actually made a lot of sense.

Then she spoiled her profound words a bit by saying, 'I think my heart is telling me to not bother chopping a lot of vegetables for you to push around your plate. It wants me to open a tin of spaghetti hoops instead.'

THURSDAY 5TH APRIL

All day I've been going back and forth, trying to make up my mind about Ethan. First, I'd imagine us hanging out saying hilarious things and no one mentioning sport. Then I'd picture trying to tell him that I liked him, and I'd see him pulling his superior face and turning me down flat. But, as I walked home from school, I thought about seeing Ethan at Juicy Lucy's tonight and my heart started pumping harder and all I could think about was that time I thought he was going to kiss me and how I really wanted him to. And how I still do.

Mum's right; I've got to go with my heart. Tonight I'm going to tell Ethan how I feel.

LATER

Before we got to Juicy Lucy's, I was trying not to overplan things with Ethan. I thought we'd have a little chat where I made him laugh and then maybe we'd lose the rest of the gang and go for a walk together, and perhaps he'd confess that all of his sarky remarks over the last couple of months have been because he was insanely jealous of Finn, and I'd tell him that I really like him. Then he'd say that my intelligence makes him weak at the knees and my smile makes him want to kiss me . . .

So no specific plan.

Totally prepared to go with the flow.

But as soon as Megs and I were inside I spotted Westy and asked, 'Where's Ethan?' before I could stop myself.

'Not sure,' Westy said. 'He's around somewhere. Do you want to sit next to me, Faith?'

'Not right now. I just need to find Ethan.'

'I could buy you something to eat. I've made

up this brilliant new snack; you take a blueberry muffin, then you add a layer of ketchup—'

'Maybe later, Westy.' I felt mean brushing him off, but now that I'd made a decision I really needed to see Ethan.

Megs was having a whispery conversation with Cameron so I scanned the tables and the queue for Ethan. The place was jammed with people from our school and the boys' school.

Megs grabbed me by the arm in an unnecessarily firm way and said, 'Let's sit down for a minute.' And she dragged me off to a quiet table by the loos.

'Listen,' she said, 'I think maybe we need to talk about Ethan a bit more.'

'Megs, you don't need to keep trying to convince me that we're well suited. I've realised that you're right.'

'I don't want you to get your hopes up too high.'

'Don't worry, I promise I'm being realistic. I'm not expecting a fairy tale; I just want to see how things go.'

I was looking over people's heads at the entrance, still waiting for Ethan to appear.

'I'm not sure he's even coming,' Megs said. She was starting to sound a bit shrill.

'Didn't he come with Cam?'

Megs hesitated in an extremely shifty way. 'You know there are some really fit Year Elevens here. Cam knows a boy who's always being rude to his teachers; you'd like him.'

'Can I sit with you two?' Westy said. 'That lot are a bit immature.'

I thought Megs was going to wave him away, but she said, 'Faith, I'm going to get you a very sugary drink and then we need to have a chat. Westy, don't let her move.'

I wasn't really listening; I was starting to panic that maybe Ethan wouldn't show.

Westy plonked himself down. 'You all right, Faith?'

'Yeah, fine.'

'Are you upset about you and Finn? I heard you split up.'

I shrugged. I actually hadn't thought about Finn for several days.

'Sorry if you're sad. But he didn't deserve you because you're … you're really nice.' Westy was squirming a bit.

'Thanks, but I'm not that bothered about Finn really.'

'That's great!' Westy grinned. 'So why are you looking worried? Why don't you tell Westy what the problem is? Go on, you know me; I'm good at keeping secrets. I'm very quiet. Hardly speak. Don't mix much. Nothing will shock me. You can say anything you like.'

I caught sight of some curly hair and my heart leapt. But it wasn't Ethan. 'It's nothing,' I said.

'Is it your love life?'

'I'm fine, Westy.'

'Maybe you're dating the wrong kind of boy. Have you thought about trying something more in the lovable bear range?'

'Very funny.'

'All that good looks and charm must get tiring after a while though, don't they?'

He looked so hopeful that I couldn't help laughing. 'If it did then we'd all go off you, wouldn't we?'

Westy coloured right up which was really very sweet. 'Er, Faith?' he said.

Elliot came past our table on the way to the loos.

'Have you seen Ethan?' I asked him.

'Yeah, he's downstairs with some St Mildred's girls.'

I stood up.

'Hang on, Faith,' Westy said. 'I wanted to ask you something.'

'I'll be back in a sec!' I called over my shoulder.

I smoothed my hair and tried to walk down the stairs in a casual yet devastatingly attractive way. Below me I could see the glossy heads of a pack of St Minger's; trust them to be cluttering up the place. I hoped that Dawn wasn't one of the ones talking to Ethan.

'Faith, wait!' Megs yelled from the top of the stairs.

But it was too late.

I'd already spotted Ethan.

And Dawn.

They weren't talking. They were kissing.

Now what am I supposed to do?